Journal of a Voyage to Australia

The epic 1855 diary of Henry Morrison,
his sea journey from England to Australia and back
and ordeal mining for Gold in country Victoria.

Illustrations by John Koulaouzos

Publisher: Inspiring Publishers,
P.O. Box 159, Calwell, ACT Australia 2905
Email: publishaspg@gmail.com
http://www.inspiringpublishers.com

A catalogue record for this book is available from the National Library of Australia

National Library of Australia The Prepublication Data Service

Author: Henry Morrison / John Koulaouzos
Title: A Journal of a Voyage to Australia
Genre: Biography, Memoir, Travel Literature
ISBN: 978-1-922327-66-6

Contents

Foreword

The journey of a
A Journal of a Voyage to Australia

Before reading my great, great grandfather's journal, it may also be of interest to the reader to know how this artifact fortunately came into my possession.

Since childhood I always recalled hearing rumours, within our family, of an old diary written by a long gone ancestor on my mother's paternal side, the Morrisons.

Unfortunately, no one in my family seemed to know the whereabouts of the book. Most likely it was hidden somewhere within the cavernous house, workshop or printing studio that made up the Morrison enclave at Bexley, a southern suburb of Sydney, Australia.

Cursory searches over the years uncovered nothing. My three elderly uncles, who lived at Bexley, didn't seem overly concerned with finding the book, or of uncovering any of our family history for that matter. I hoped it was a case of indifference and not of keeping skeletons hidden in the closet.

Over the years my uncles sadly passed on, leaving behind a dilapidated house, workshop and printing studio full to the brim with personal possessions, books, magazines, photos, old furniture and flotsam and jetsam gathered over generations.

As my uncles had no other surviving family members living in Australia, it was left for me to sort, clean, repair and save any items of importance to our family found at the property.

In 2009 I began the arduous task, which would take almost a year to complete. Thankfully I had the help of a friend, Terry Stevens, to ease the job and boredom of sorting and removing the contents from such a large premises. Whilst working and talking,

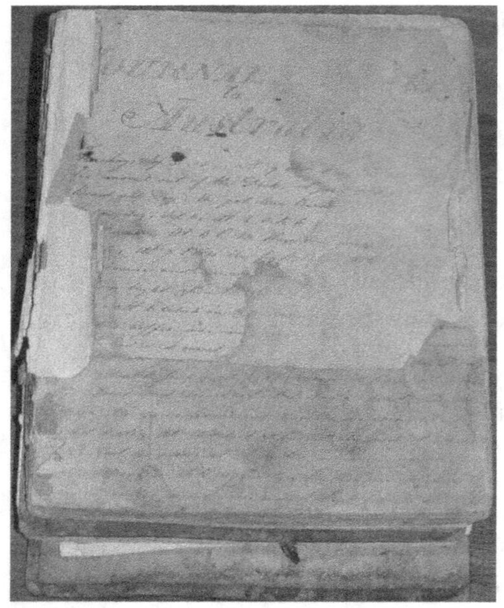

I mentioned to Terry the legend of the diary, so that he may be aware and not inadvertently dispose of it.

Less than a few days after our talk, we were working our way through large piles of magazines and documents in the front print shop when Terry casually called out to me "here's the diary".

He then handed me a very old, worn out small book with rotten, water stained pages and the simple hand written title on the front cover "Journal of a Voyage to Australia". I couldn't believe it. The lost treasure had been found!

Terry had discovered the diary under a pile of dusty magazines sitting on my uncle's work desk next to the shop front.

Unfortunately the desk was next to a large, rotten wood framed window which exposed the book to harsh sunlight and the occasional water leak. It was regrettable that a book, which for over 150 years had withstood the harsh conditions of countless travels around the world and being handed down from generation to generation, was left to deteriorate under a pile of worthless magazines.

Luckily, despite the books rough treatment, most of my ancestor's memoir was still legible, and so I undertook another major task: transcribing the handwritten notes to print.

It proved a more difficult job than I had imagined, as the ink had faded on many of the water damaged pages. To help with legibility, I scanned every page of the diary and computer processed them in a different tone at a higher contrast.

My ancestor's unique cursive writing style also took time to comprehend. In many instances I had to assume the intent of sentences, or even individual words, whilst still keeping as accurate to the original text as possible. I eventually became adept at deciphering his writing.

Original journal page

Processed journal page

After a year, I was successful in copying the entire diary to electronic text so that this important historical document would be preserved and accessible. The thoughts, observations and experiences of a traveller from 150 years ago could now be easily shared with a modern reader, to partly understand what life was like during that era.

I have included my own illustrations to the book as a light hearted, modern interpretation of moments experienced by Henry.

I hope my ancestor approves.

John Elliot Koulaouzos
Great, great grandson of Henry Morrison

Journal of a
Voyage to Australia

Departing from England

Tuesday, Sep 5 **1854**. At 9 o'clock, in the morning, we moved out of the Dock. A good deal of us had been on board all day. We got our berths first.

Wednesday, Sept 6. At 2 o'clock a gale blew before dinner. At 4 pm there was a preaching. At 7pm we had tea. Afterwards there was music and dancing.

At 6 o'clock in the morning we had breakfast. The coffee was ready, which I smelt from bed and woke me.

The coast about 70 miles, she left us at 9pm.

Had a good breeze, which set us along at 7 knots per hour. As the steam boat passed us there was a great cheering. There were a good few letters sent by the steamer for to be posted for friends.

Sept 9th Sick all day, like many more.

Sept 10th Weather dull. Still sick. Today, Sunday. Devine sermon on board, conducted by the Captain.

Sept 11th Still sick today. We saw a shoal of porpoises.

Sept 12th. Sick, and not much interested to eat.

Sept 13th. We had the first squall of wind, today. Sipped some water. It was a good treat. I am a good deal better today.
Sea becalmed nearly all day. Weather a little damp.

Sept 15th A good breeze with rain, which continued. Wet weather disagreeable on shipboard. A fine day of strong breeze blowing.
In the evening the bagpipes were played, and some parties were dancing. All appear to be happy.

Sep 20th We are still becalmed this morning.
At 3 o'clock, in the afternoon, a breeze picking up, and sent us along at the rate of 9½ knots.
At 4 o'clock we passed two vessels. One of them, a Spaniard, hoisted his flag, but our Captain did not return the compliment.

Sept 21st Our ship rolled very much last night, making all sorts of crockery rattle about in a furious manner. We are going along about 10 knots today.
Notice put up that all washing be done Mondays and Thursdays, as to keep the decks as tidy as possible.

Sep 22nd Ship still running at a good rate today. We had a real hardy tea of hot cake and butter. Farther on, in the night, all sorts of gossip going on, while the sailors are jumping and singing their sea songs.

All on board seem to be satisfied

Sep 23rd Weather fine. A light shower of rain at 12 noon. At 5 we saw a vessel at a distance ahead. She was heading the same course as us. We are going at a good rate.

At 10 o'clock, at night, we had a squall which set us along at 12 knots.

The weather still squally. Farther on in the day, the weather more moderate. We go at 8 knots.
At night we were becalmed.

The Cook taken ill, with cramp in the stomach.

Sep 25th A fine clear morning. Very little wind. I had a small washing. Got the things well dried. Cook better today. At night we were becalmed. Air very close.

Sep 26th A fine day. Weather very warm. Becalmed all day. Music and dancing upon deck.

Sep 27th We are still becalmed. Weather very warm. A good many of the passengers lay upon the floors and tables, last night, on account of the heat.

At 4 o'clock this morning I had a bath in a large tub full of water. Felt very much refreshed after it.

At 6 pm a light breeze sprung up.

Sep 28th All but becalmed this morning. Weather very warm. 80 degree (27C) in the shade. We are all very healthy so far.

Sep 29th A fine day. Ship going at 7 knots. We saw a large vessel about 4 miles off. She was a steam ship. They hoisted their flag, and ours was hoisted in reply.

At night the moon shinning bright upon the restless sea. Plenty of gossip upon deck.

Sep 30th I slept on the table last night. Did not sleep very well, as the ship rolled very much. At half past 3am I went upon deck and got a drink, after which I felt very comfortable. Ship going at 6 knots. Weather fine and clear.

Oct 1st Rather cloudy this morning. We have got the trade winds. We are going at 8 knots. There are a great many swallows about the ship. There have been some caught by the passengers, and set at liberty again. There are a good many flying fish about the ship. They fly very quick. They fly a long way without alighting.

Today we are in the tropics.

The weather is not very warm as there is a fine breeze. At night weather very cloudy.

Oct 2nd Weather still very cloudy. We sighted Cape De Verd Islands at 7am. They were at 15 miles distant from us.

Farther on in the day the weather cleared up, so we had a good view of them. They appeared to be very high land.

We saw four large vessels. Our Captain said he thought they were American whalers, bound for the South Sea fisheries.

At night a good many bathers in the large tub.

Oct 3rd Weather very fine. We saw a vessel homeward bound. Our Captain, and the Captain of the other vessel, signalled one to another, but us passengers did not understand it. We were going along at 7½ knots. At night weather very cloudy.

Oct 4th Last night a good many passengers lay upon deck, the air been so close and warm between decks.

Today the passengers and Captain had a dispute about the quantity of water allowed to each passenger. The excuse the Captain made was that the casks sent on board by the agent were deficient by 40 gallons each.

At 4 pm there was meeting of the passengers to adopt measures for prosecuting the Captain if he did not give the full quantity to each. The resolution came to were, that six of the passengers be chosen to lay the grievances before the proper authorities, and that a fund be raised to defray the law expenses if necessary.

Today weather squally, with a little rain. At night there was a little lightning.

At 8pm a meeting was called among the passengers to take into consideration the next method of keeping the 'tween decks clean. It was agreed that each on give sixpence. The money thus raised amounted to five pounds. It was then agreed that 4 men be elected to do the work, and receive the money when they got at the end of the voyage.

Oct 5th I lay under the table last night. Slept till 2am. When I went upon deck, a good breeze blowing. Ship going at 9½ knots. Stayed on deck an hour and half, then went down to bed again where I lay till 6am.

There is not much rest for those who are not used to sea life.

In the afternoon we were becalmed. Saw a large shoal of porpoises.

We expect to reach the Line[1] by Sunday, if the winds are fair, but they are very uncertain about these latitudes.

This afternoon there was a meeting to elect the men to clean the 'tween decks. There were seven candidates up for the job, but only four were elected. The proceedings were carried through, in regular election style. All parties seem to enjoy these meetings.

Tonight, weather cloudy. The moon shooting stray beams through, now and then.

There are all sorts of gymnastics going forward, such as climbing the ropes, jumping, wrestling and the like. All these things tend to keep us healthy.

---

[1] The equator

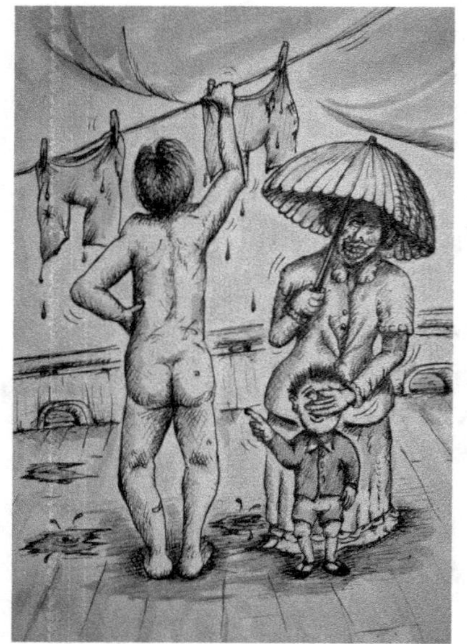

Oct 6th Becalmed early all day. Had some heavy showers.

Oct 7th I lay in a hammock through the night. Slept very well, but the rain came down the hatchway and wet one end of the hammock and clothes.
This morning very dull and wet. There is a light breeze, but it is against us. Things going on through the day, as usual.

Oct 8th A fine morning. At 10pm we had a squall with rain. I had a small washing. Got them dried. In the afternoon weather very changeable.

Oct 9th This morning, at half past 4 pm, I had a bath. Weather very squally through the day. At night ship running at 10 knots.

Oct 10th We have been sailing very well last night, but a little out of our course. We continued so all today.

Oct 11th Things going on as usual. All hands healthy.

Oct 12th We are going a little this morning. Some of the passengers are getting ready for the dress for Neptune[2], but the most of the passengers are against the system as the proceedings are so rough when most gentlemen comes on board ship. This evening we had a beautiful sunset, such as we never see in the Northern latitudes.
This is by far the most pleasant part of the day. It seems to infuse new life into all on board, after the excessive heat of the day time.

Oct 13th Weather very fine. Ship going slowly. Wind right ahead of us. Ship out of her course.

A death at sea

Oct 14th I slept in a hammock last night.

This afternoon, at 2 o'clock, one of the crew fell from the foreyard sail to the deck. A distance of 122 feet. He was all broken to pieces. He died almost instantly. At five o'clock he was launched into the deep, blue sea. It was a sad sight. A man who was in good health at noon to be drift into the sea at 5 the same day.
All on board were much affected.

---

[2] The Neptune ceremony is an age old tradition to initiate travellers crossing the equator by sea for the first time, usually with a high ranking seaman dressed as King Neptune, and the others in similar mythical costume.

Oct 15th Ship going nearer her course. Weather fine. We crossed the Line today with a good breeze, which made it very pleasant.

Oct 16th This morning at half past 3 o'clock, as they were putting the ship about, a block struck the mate on the head and knocked him down. Farther on in the day, one of the crew had his hand hurt by a block falling upon it from aloft.

At half past 3 o'clock in the afternoon, as they were tacking ship, one of the crew held too long on one of the ropes, which caused the maint of gallant yard to snap right in two. The sailors were soon up at work, clearing away the wreck. They got it down a little after dark.

Oct 17th A fine morning. A good breeze. At 4 o'clock the sailors had another yard up, and the sail upon it. Today we saw a small island, distant about 5 miles to windward of us. It was near the coast of South America. It is named Fernand De Narmala. There are a great quantity of birds upon this island. A good many come flying

around the ship. There were some of them shot, but they fell into the water. We saw a small whale at a distance.

It was blowing the water up at a great height. These sights break the monotony of sea life.

Oct 19th This morning we have a good breeze. At 11am we saw the South American Coast. This place is called Pernambuco.

We saw a good many boats or rafts. They appeared to be fishing. They are very curiously put together. They appear to be a lot of spars lashed together and buoyed up with cork.

At 2 o'clock, this afternoon, we saw a large shoal of porpoises. They were sporting about very near the ship. Some of them spring a great distance. They sported about a long time. At last, some of them came right across the ship's bow. The boatswain was already with the harpoon. When one came within reach he aimed, and passed the harpoon right through one. He struggled very much and bent the harpoon.

After it was hauled upon deck, two of the crew commenced to skin it. After this they took out the entrails, which are formed very much like a swine. The skin, in some parts of the body, is ¾ of an inch thick.

This one was about 12 stones weight (76kg), and measured 7 feet long. Several parties had a chop of it, which tasted not far amiss when pepper and salt were added plentifully.

Oct 20th We have been going very well through last night. We are going on as usual today. Weather fine.

Oct 21st At 4 o'clock, this morn, ship going at 12 knots. Ship is pitching a little. At 3 in the afternoon the wind fell back, but freshened last night.

Oct 22nd Last night a flying fish flew on board. Been chased by a dolphin. They are about 12in long. The fins are winged, and are 6in long. This morning ship going well, till 12 o'clock when the breeze slackened. Wind freshened at night.
The weather is fine. Not too hot.

Oct 23rd This morning we saw a large ship, on our weather quarter. She was going the same course, but we soon left her a long way astern. Farther on in the day we saw another vessel ahead. She was going the same course as us. At 2pm we passed a large vessel very close. Our Captain hailed her, and asked where from, and where bound to. Her name was the Cutter of Newhaven, North America. She was from Calais and bound to St Thomas's in the West Indies. After all questions were asked and answered, each vessel sheared off to her right course. All on board were highly gratified at having passed a vessel so close.
The weather at this time was very fine.

Oct 24th Today we passed an island, named Trindade, Lat 21° 30" South Lon 29° West. It is not inhabited. The Sun appears to set very quick in these latitudes. After she disappears, below the horizon, there are some of the most beautiful colours reflected upon the clear, blue sky.

Oct 25th We are going very slow today. In the evening there was music and dancing upon deck. These meetings help to pass the time away.

Oct 26th We have been going rather better, through the night. But, we are going as slow as ever, this morning. The sky seems to be loaded with rain. At night the weather turned very rough, and rained very heavy. This sent most of the passengers below. Some of them commenced to sing, some to play at cards, others to reading and conversing, but the singing carried the sway, as most all were for something lively.

Oct 27th Ship pitched about very much, last night. The weather still stormy, but not wet. The ship is rather out of her course. At 12am a ship ahead, but not seen very distinctly. Our Captain set more sail. We passed her at 8 o'clock. We going at 12 knots. This gave great satisfaction to all on board.

Oct 28th This morning the vessel nearly out of sight astern. We are sailing our right course, at 10 knots per hour. This weather is rather cold this morning. The wind kept good all day.

Oct 29th We have been going very quick in the night. We still have a fine breeze, and a clear blue sky. At 10am there was divine service upon deck. In the afternoon one of the passengers preached between decks.

Oct 30th The weather is delightful this morning. Farther on in the day, the boatswain caught a porpoise. We have been going at 10 knots per hour all day. At night music and dancing.

Oct 31st Ship going very slow this morning. The sky is very much overcast. There are a good many different kinds of birds following the ship. At 7am we saw a sail at great distance ahead. She was going the same course as us. At 10am we passed her. Shortly after we passed the vessel, we saw a shoal of bottle nosed whales.

The smaller fish (such as porpoises and the like) had to flee before them. At night music and dancing upon deck.

Nov 1st We saw a great number of birds, this morning. Farther on in the day we passed a large vessel going the same course as us. We have passed all the vessels we have seen, since we commenced the voyage. Today passed an island at a distance. It is 800 feet high. It was capped with snow, which shone beautifully in the sun. The air is cold, but very clear and healthy.

Nov 2ⁿᵈ We are sailing our right course, at 11knots per hour. The sea is rolling in our favour. Weather very cold at night. The moon shining very brightly.

Nov 3ʳᵈ Today weather very cloudy. A large number of Cape Pigeons, about the ship. We are going at 11 knots. Today one of the passengers took a fit, in which he fell with great force upon the deck. He appeared to be a strong, healthy man.

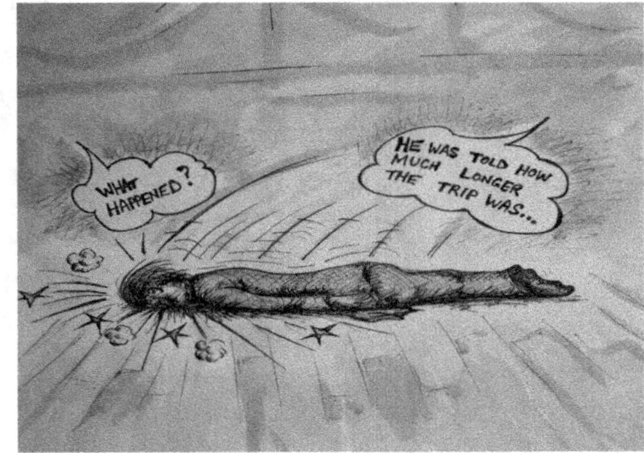

Nov 4ᵗʰ Weather still cloudy. Ship sailing very well, today. At night ship going 13 knots.

Nov 5ᵗʰ Weather cloudy and damp. Ship going slow. At night a breeze sprung up, which set us along at 8 knots per hour.

Nov 6ᵗʰ A strong breeze, but not very favourable. Farther on the day, weather very squally.

Nov 7ᵗʰ Wind blowing hard all day. At night, very dark. Neither moon, nor stars, visible. There is a strong sea running. There are a few persons sick for the first time, since leaving the Irish Channel, but otherwise we are very healthy.

Nov 8ᵗʰ Wind as fresh as ever. Sea not quite high. Ship rather out of our course. The weather is very clear, and healthy. Toward night the wind fell, just as the sun was setting. We caught a Cape Pigeon. They are the about the size of an ordinary pigeon. They are not able to rise on the wind, unless they are in the water.
The weather very cold.

Nov 9th We are becalmed today. There are a good many parties trying to catch birds, with the fishing line and hook. A good many of the birds picked at the bait, but swam off as soon as they felt the hook. Some of them got fast, and were drawn very near the ship, but they soon got off when they were being drawn up from the water.

The one we caught, the day before, we set free. He seemed to prize liberty very much. He flew right out of sight without ever looking behind.

Tonight we had a very fine sunset. It was almost worth coming this far to see.

There is a heavy dew falling, after sunset, which soon wets the clothes through

Nov 10th A good breeze this morning. We are going our right course. Weather rather, rather dull, and very cold. At night music and dancing upon deck.

Nov 11th We are going very slow this morning. Wind ahead.

Today we have the allowance of four articles reduced:

tea, sugar, butter and flour.

Weather very warm.

Nov 12th Wind still rather ahead. Ship going a little quickly. Weather not so cold, this morning.

Nov 13th We are becalmed, this morning. The Captain intends calling at the Cape of Good Hope, where he intends getting a supply of provisions. All the passengers are in great glee, as they expect to get on shore.
Farther on in the day we get a breeze, which carried us along at 9 knots. We are not far from the Cape.
All is ready for the ship coming to an anchorage, when we get into Table Bay. At night the sky very clear. The stars shining, like diamonds on the sea.

A stop at the Cape of Good Hope

Nov 14th At 5am we sighted land. The weather pleasant, in the extreme. All of us are in good spirits. A good many parties are already dressed for going on shore. As soon as we got near the land, the wind fell and we were becalmed, but there is a strong current setting in toward the bay.

At 3pm the anchor was dropped, right opposite the town. The sight of which is very fine. There were a good many vessels. Thrice of which were emigrant ships.

One of them, named the James McHenry, left Liverpool ten days before us.

Another left sixteen days before us. Both these vessels had just put in for provisions. When we got on shore we heard that the passengers were very badly accommodated, on board both these vessels.

The town is situated in a cove,

close to the waters edge. All the buildings are whitewashed, and have trees of one kind or other growing before them. Some of the buildings have vines growing up the front. It is a very pleasant place.

In the background there is Table Mountain, which rises to the height of 3700 feet above the level of the sea.

As soon as we saw through the principal streets, we went to the botanical gardens, which are open to strangers and travellers. This sight was very refreshing after being on the sea so long.

There were a good many English house plants growing in the open air, such as fusions, geraniums, scarlet hummers and the like. The only tropical fruits growing were the date, fig, pomegranate, banana and melon.

In the centre of the garden there was an artificial lake, with a fountain in the centre which was shooting up a spire of clean water. There were some gold and silver fishes sporting in the crestal lake.

After enjoying this sight for a while, we made the best of our way to seek lodgings, which we got for a shilling a head.

Nov 15th This morning we rose early and strolled up the hills, in the neighbourhood of the town. The height of these hills were about 1100 feet above the sea level. The view from the top was very fine. After a while we made the best of our way down to the town to look after some breakfast, as the mountain air gave us a keen appetite which we satisfied with mutton chops and coffee, for one shilling each.

There were 1200 passengers on shore, from different ships. Wine, tobacco and spirits are very cheap. The wine is from 4 shilling per bottle. Tobacco from 1 shilling. Fruit was not very cheap. We purchased a few articles of provision, to use on the remainder of the voyage. After having another look through the town we went down to the landing stage, to get a boat to take us on board the ship.

There are a good many boats always ready. We pay 6 shilling each for the passage to the ship, which was lying about a mile and half from the shore.

After we got on board we got things put in order, as all our ships cloths were lying about the berth, as we had not time to side away before going ashore.

There are a good many of both sailors and passengers drunk, and unruly.

All will be right in a day or two, we expect.

Nov 16th The sails are set, and the anchor weighed. We are only waiting for a breeze. There is one of the passengers missing. Farther on in the day, the missing man came on board, just as the ship was getting under way.

At night the Captain's cook put in irons for being drunk, and threatening to stab one of the passengers. After the irons were put on he attempted to jump overboard, but the mate got hold of him and sent him to a secure place.

Nov 17th We are going very well this morning. Weather very fine. At night music and dancing upon deck. Ship rolling a little.

Nov 18th Weather very dull. A head wind. Ship pitching a little. At night weather more stormy.

Nov 19th The wind blew very hard through last night. Ship tossed about very much. Part of one of the jibs blown away. The weather is very stormy this morning. Farther on in the day, weather more moderate. This afternoon the wind came fair. This put us all in good spirits. There is a ship ahead, going the same course as us.
At 3pm divine service below, by one of the passengers.

Nov 20th A fine clear morning, but very little wind. The vessel, still in sight. Toward the latter part of the day lost sight of her. At night we had a squall, and a heavy shower of rain.

Nov 21st Ship rolling very much, but going at a good speed. At 7pm it rained very heavy. After a while the weather more moderate, but soon more rain came with a heavy squall of wind.
A good many of us got wet, with the sea coming over the ship. A great quantity of water came down between the decks. Weather kept squally all day.

Nov 22nd Wind and sea as high as ever. Ship going very well. Affairs going on as usual.

Nov 23rd Ship tossed about very much through last night. We were like to have been thrown out of bed.
A many slept on the tables. This morning the weather is very clear, sea very rough. Ship is still going as quick as before. At night the wind slackened a little.

Nov 24th Weather more moderate this morning. The sea is a good deal calmer.

At 12 noon we were going very slow. At night the wind freshened, and set us along at 11 knots per hour.

Nov 25th We are going very slow this morning, but at 1pm we got a strong breeze, accompanied by heavy rain. This weather continued all day.

Nov 26th Today the weather is very rough, and squally. There is a strong sea running, which causes the ship to roll, and pitching very much. This afternoon one of our mess mates fell down the ladder, and hurt his knee very much.

There has been a great quantity of water come on board, and down

between the decks. At night the hatches were put on, and battened down, as the Captain expected some very rough weather before morning.

Nov 27th We had a very rough night. Some very heavy seas struck the ship, which trembled from stern to stern. This morning, at 2 o'clock, a passenger was found washing about the deck by the force of the water, which had come upon deck.

He had gone up late the night before, while he was the worse for drink. When picked up he was quite insensible. However, he was bought about in a short time. There was nine inches of water on the saloon floor.

There was also a large quantity of water washing about between decks, and in the berths, making the place not over comfortable.

No 28th Weather not quite so rough this morning, but the ship is rolling very much, setting the breakfast things to rattle about from side to side.

There is very little chance of walking without taking hold of something. There are some droll sights upon deck, at times, such as a lot of women washing clothes.

When the ship will give an extra lurch, which sends women and washing tubs down into the lee-scuppers[3]. One of the women, in particular, got a good treat for, after slipping down upon the deck, she upset a large tub full of water upon herself, and slipped down into the lee-scuppers.

At this sight the others laughed like to split their sides.

The most of us have tried whether the deck for ourselves is the hardest. Sometimes, when the ship gives a heavy roll, it sets a lot of us slipping across the deck at full speed and, if not lucky enough to get hold, we go back again as fast as we came.

All of these sights cause much laughter among the others.

Ship going at 12 knots. We expect to see some islands in a day or two.

---

[3] Lee-scuppers are numerous large drainage points situated along the inside edge of the ship's deck to allow water to drain off the side.

Nov 29th A fine breeze. Ship going gaily along at 10 knots. Weather delightful. At night we were going very smooth, and steady. The moon shining bright, in the clear blue sky, and reflecting her silvery rays upon the deep, blue sea.

There was a lecture between decks tonight upon the future rewards, and punishments. These lectures help to break the monotony of sea life.

Nov 30th We are going along as usual. Weather still fine, this morning. I washed a few clothes. We are sailing at 11 knots.

At 8pm we saw a curious sight. It consisted of a meteor shooting towards the horizon, at the same moment a flash of lightning passed along the sky while, on the opposite side of the heavens, the moon was shining brightly.

Music and dancing upon deck.

Dec 1st We are still going along at a good speed. Weather very clear and cool. The wind is from the south east. Farther on in the day, the wind came from the south, which caused it to be very cold. At night the Moon shone bright overhead.

Fight with the cook

Dec 2nd We are going along as usual. Toward night there was a fight on board between the Captain's cook (who is a Spaniard), and one of the passengers. The cook accused him of stealing a loaf of bread. The passenger denied it, however they got to fighting.

After they had fought a while, the Captain came. When the cook went into the galley, the Captain got hold of the passenger, and struck him in the face. At this the whole of the passengers, that were collected, cried out "shame upon the Captain!".

Just as they had done this, the cook rushed out of the galley with a knife in his hand threatening to stab the passenger.

At this fearful threat the passengers shouted "overboard with the cook!", but the man had got out of the way or he would have been stabbed. After this, the passengers went to the Captain and desired him to put the cook in irons[4], as he still threatened the other one's life. But the Captain would not agree to this proposal.

Today, two articles short in our provision : potatoes and suet. The passengers were much surprised to hear that the provisions were short again, as the Captain gave his word of honour that he would put sufficient stores on board, at the Cape, for the remainder of the voyage.

The salted flesh we got on board is hardly fit to eat. The butter is also very bad. As to cheese, he would not get any as he said it was too dear. The most of the passengers are for appealing to the law for redress, when we get to Melbourne, which we expect to reach in about a fortnight's time. At present we are in the Indian Ocean, midway between the Cape and Melbourne.

---

[4] a common term of the time meaning to restrain with metal hand or leg shackles.

Dec 3rd We are not going quite so fast this morning, but the weather is extremely pleasant.
We have passed the island of St Pauls and Amsterdam, some time through last night. These islands lie in Lat 39º South, Lon 77º 55" East

Dec 4th Weather rather cloudy this morning. Farther on in the day the wind came ahead but, at night, the wind came fair and freshened up to a stiff breeze, which sent us along at the rate of 11 knots. Air very cold.

This morning a porpoise caught. It was soon cut up to be eaten. There was a good many of them sporting around the ship, beside a large quantity of small whales known by the name of bottled nose whales.

This afternoon there was a shooting match upon deck for £1 a side.

A birth at sea

Dec 5th A good breeze this morning. Sometime through last night there was a birth on board.
Weather very cold. Things going on as usual. At night weather very damp.

Dec 6th Breeze still holds good. A little rain, wind cold.

Dec 7th Weather stormy and wet. Ship going well. There are a good many different kinds of birds following the ship. Some of them are of fine plumage .

Dec 8th Weather fine this morning with a fine breeze. Ship going freely along at 11 knots. All parties are in good spirits, as we expect to be in Melbourne in a week or so.
At 2 o'clock the breeze got stronger, which continued all day.

Dec 9th Wind not so high this morning. At 8pm we passed a small vessel going the same course as us. Weather cold and clear.
Dec 10th Wind ahead this morning. Weather very cold and squally, accompanied with showers of sleet. At night the wind freshened up, and came more favourable. At 10 o'clock we were going at 13 knots per hour.

Dec 12th We are nearly becalmed this morning. Weather fine and mild all day.

Dec 13th We are going a little better this morning. Sea very calm. Subscriptions are been made for the inspector of the cleaning department, and another for the doctor.
At night the wind freshened up a good deal. Ship going at 12 knots, at 10 o'clock.

Dec 14th We are going on very quick this morning. Weather very cold. Ship going very steady. There are a good many parties getting their luggage ready for going on shore.
At 1pm a child died. It has been ill a long time. Farther on in the day the wind came ahead. The sea got very high by night.

Dec 15th Ship rolled and pitched very much last night, beside going very slow.
The parents, belonging the dead child, wish to rest it till we reach Melbourne, so as they may bury it on shore. The Captain allowed them to put it in the quarter boat.
At night the sea lowered a little.

Dec 16th Soon on this morning the weather turned very squally. In the first squall ship running at 14 knots. The sea ran very high all day. Toward night the starboard quarter boat, which contained the dead child, was washed away.

After a while weather more calm and clear.

Dec 17th Weather fine. A light breeze. Ship going at 7 knots.

Dec 18th Ship going at 11 knots. Today commenced to get the anchor ready. At night a good many looking out for Cape Otway lights.

About 11 o'clock, at night, a great disturbance between decks by a lot of the passengers kicking tin pans, and the like, about. After this game had gone on for some time, the second mate and boatswain brought the hand shackle down.

They caught one party in the act

of kicking a tin pan. The mate got hold of him, and was about to put the hand shackle on. At this there was a complete uproar of hissing and shouting.

However, the mate let the man go. After that the passengers were quiet, and retired to bed.

Air very clear and cold.

Arrival in Melbourne, Australia

Dec 19th This morning, at 6am, we sighted land, which put all in good spirits. Weather fine. Ship going at 12 knots, with a fine breeze from south. At 5 in the evening the pilot came on board. All passengers were cleared of the quarter deck. At 6 o'clock we were safely over the bar, and within Port Phillip Heads.

We layed too, till the inspector and doctor came on board. The inspector asked if we had any provisions short of the allowance agreed for. All, with one accord, shouted yes.

The inspector left the ship.

The sails were trimmed and we proceeded up Hobsons Bay, at the rate of 14 knots per hour for a good many miles. There was a ship going the same way, but we passed her like a shot. She was an old bluff, slow and sure.

Weather very fine. Tonight are rather warm between decks. This is caused with been in under the land.

At 11pm we anchor 7 miles below Williams Town, which is 9 miles below Melbourne.

Dec 20th At 4am the anchor was weighed and we proceeded towards the shipping. There we brought up. There are a large number of the largest vessels. Some taken in cargo, others delivering.

We expected to get on shore today, but were disappointed as the Captain did not get the ship cleared at the customs till late in the day. There is a great confusion between deck. All the luggage been out of the berths, while everyone is bustling about and getting ready for going on shore as soon as possible.

Dec 21ˢᵗ All the luggage was on board the lighter boat by 12 o'clock in the day, at which time we were very soon speeding up the river Yarra Yarra,[5] which is only a narrow stream averaging about 30 yards. It's banks are low and wooded on each side, for a few miles up, with low trees.

After landing on the wharf, at Melbourne, we sought out lodgings where we conveyed our luggage. The lodgings we got, we had to pay 30 shillings per week for.

There were 2 small rooms very much out of refrain, with no furniture of any sought, but there was no scarcity of rats.

There was seven of us together. All thought of going to the diggings, if we could not get employment in Melbourne.

Dec 22ⁿᵈ We went down to Williams Town, to be present at the court, as the Captain was summoned to appear to answer the charge of short allowance in the provision. The magistrate advised the Captain to compromise, if the passengers would, so it was agreed that the passengers should receive two pounds each, as compensation.

As soon as we received our money, we proceeded up to Melbourne, where we arrived in the evening.

Dec 23ʳᵈ We sought the parties out, whom we had letters for. They lived in Collingwood, which is about 2 miles from Melbourne. Things were very dull in Melbourne. We could not get a job of any kind.

---

[5] Originally thought to be the Aboriginal name for the river, but actually a native word for small waterfall. Now known simply as the Yarra River.

Dec 24th We had another look around the town. It is a fine place. About the outskirts there are some fine park like scones, but the grass is not very green, owing to the heat and dryness of the soil. The water is only middling, and is rather warm, which makes it worse. The weather is very hot, especially in the narrow streets and lanes.

Dec 25th Today, Christmas. All business is suspended.

We have posted a letter for England. We saw a good many of the passengers. They intend going off to the diggings, as that seems the only resort for a living. We had a good dinner, of roast beef and plumb pudding, at an eating house. We paid 1s "6 each. The name of the house is Live and Let live.

Off to Forest Creek

Dec 26th Started today, at 12 o'clock, for the diggings at Forest Creek. Distant about 80 miles from Melbourne. Our luggage was in a dray. At 7 o'clock we camped for the night, having travelled about 20 miles. The place encamped in was a piece of enclosed ground, on private property. After we had tea, we got our tent rigged up. It consisted of the tarpaulin, belonging to the dray. We put it over the shafts of the dray. We lay under this very comfortable till morning.

Dec 27th After breakfast, we commenced to jog, as through a fine county. We met a good many bullock drays, laden with wool. We passed a good number of dead bullocks, by the way side. At about 7 o'clock we came into the entrance of the black forest. It got this name through an immense fire, which burned nearly all the grass, and a great number of trees, beside blackening the remainds.

We encamped here for the night.

It was a curious sight, when the fire was lit. It threw strange shadows around among the dismal looking old trees. After we had dispatched supper (which we were in good time for), we prepared our tent as before.

George had his hammock slung between two trees for the night.

Dec 28th After making a hearty breakfast, we started to jog on through the forest. It is about 12 miles long. The roads through the forest are very indifferent. After getting through the forest, the roads were much better, so that we got a little faster on. Toward night, the weather turned very rough and wet.

We were soon wet to the skin. We had a poor prospect for camping, so it turned out for the night was very wet and stormy, and a good soaking we got before morning.

We had a large fire on but, when the heaviest of the rain, it was drowned out in a few minutes. This made things look very dismal, however we got the night passed over.

Dec 29th We rose early and got a fire on, as best we could with damp wood. After we breakfasted, three of us started on the road, leaving our other mates and the dray to follow as soon as the road should dry a little.

We travelled on to Forest Creek, where we had a look around among the diggings. At night we lodged with a Newcastle man. He was very kind to us. He gave us a good tea, and a bed, free of charge.

Dec 30th We rose early and walked about 2 miles farther up the road, to a place named Castlemaine. A small town.

We had a stroll around this place. By this time our other mates and the dray came up. We soon had our luggage off the dray, and laid on the ground.

We were now at a stand still, not knowing which way to turn our course for the best. However, we bought a tent and pitched it near at hand, till we looked a little farther round among the diggings.

At night we stretched ourselves upon the ground, and slept sound till morning.

Dec 31st Today Sunday we did little else but rest, and arrange small affairs for commencing to dig the next day.

Jan 1st (1855) Today, New Years Day. We unrigged our tent and removed to about 2 miles farther up the country, to a place named Campbells Creek on Flat. We soon had our tent set up. After which we set off into the bush to get some wood for digging purpose, such as windlasses and the like.

We got all ready for a start next day.

The gold dig begins

Jan 2nd We commenced to dig for gold. Three of our party were trying an old hole, while two of us were sinking a new one. They got a little out of the old one.

Jan 3rd We got to the bottom of the new hole, which was about 18 feet deep, but we could not work it owing to the water making so fast. So

this was a failure first going off, but old diggers think nothing of these things.

Our other mates are getting a small matter out of the old hole, but not what will pay working it.

Things are not quite so bright as we expected.

Jan 4th Today things going on as usual. Weather very warm.

Jan 5th One of our party tired of the small returns from digging, so he intends trying his luck at his own trade in Melbourne and, if he does not succeed, he will ship right off for England.

Jan 7th Today our partner left us, intending to proceed to town.

Then, were four of us left. We then shared off. George and me went together.

We had not as much as would purchase tools to dig with, so we went off to Castlemaine to try and get a job of work, so as to raise the means of buying tools, but we could not succeed. We did not know what to do, or which way to turn, as we were fairly hard up.

However, we came to the decision of selling our spare clothes and tools, to raise as much money as to give us a start in the digging line. We got underway. We got as much gold as paid for the days rituals. This gave us a little better heart.

Jan 8th Today Sunday. We did little but rest and talk over our future prospects. The weather is too hot for walking far.

Jan 9th We still continued on with the old place, still getting a little gold. We stuck to this hole till we were forced to give it up, on account of it not paying for working.

We went into another, which was not much better. We tried it a short while, then gave it up also. We got another, which seemed to promise a little better.

We continued in this for a time.

Jan 13th We sold the gold we had obtained in the past week. We received £2"12"0. At this rate, we were 10 shillings each clear. We thought this was a good beginning.

Jan 14th Weather fine. There has been no rain, excepting a few drops, since we came to the diggings.

George gets sick

Jan 17th Today George is disabled with dysentery. It is very prevalent among new comers. It is very often produced by drinking much cold water, when the body is over heated.

Jan 18th Weather hot. George very much prostrated by the complaint.

Jan 19th Weather very warm. Our claim is not yielding as much as will pay. Got another claim, which promised a little better.

Jan 20th George very ill. Got some arrow root for him, but this had no effect in stopping the complaint. We next tried some castor oil, which did him a little good.

In the afternoon I went to Castlemaine and sold the produce of our weeks works, for which we received £7"2"6.

Jan 21st Weather very warm. In the evening cool, and pleasant.

Jan 22nd Weather not so warm. I am laid of work with a bruised hand.

Jan 23rd George a little better today. Weather very hot.

Jan 25th This is about the hottest day we have had since we came into the colony. The heat is not less than 100 Deg in the shade. There is one privilege, and that is plenty of good water, close at hand, to quench the ever craven thirst.
Jan weather very clear, and hot.
George is about clear of the dysentery, but very weak.

Jan 29th Today our other mates left us, and went to a place about 7 miles off, to put up and work a puddling machine[6].

---

[6] a large, water filled trough that a horse drawn paddle would rotate through, to separate hard clays from gravel, to reduce the amount of fine panning, and cradling, to recover the gold.

Jan 30th Weather very dull in the morning. In the afternoon we got a supply of firewood in. Toward night it commenced to rain rather heavy. Our tent not waterproof. But, the water soon stopped coming through when the cotton swelled.

Jan 31st Weather cool and damp in the morning. After dinner, the weather cleared up. George started work.

Just as he was drawing up the first bucket of stuff, the rope broke and down went the bucket, and knocked the bottom out.
We bought another rope and bucket. They cost 10 shillings.
Got very little gold today.

Feb 1st Weather very pleasant. Gold very scarce with us. My hand is a good deal better. There are a good many parties who have bruised hands. It is mostly caused with not been used to this kind of work.

Feb 2nd George about 12 divots of gold today.

Feb 3rd Weather still very pleasant. Got about 7 divots of gold today. After dinner we went to Castlemaine and sold our gold, for which we received £3"18"0, been at the rate £3"15"0 per ounce.
We saw two of our shipmates. They were both trying the diggings. We bought some articles to make beer of. They cost 4 shillings. I posted a newspaper for England. The name of the paper was The Melbourne Weekly Age, dated Feb 3, 1855.

Feb 4th Sunday. Weather fine. We managed to raise a spice pudding for dinner. The dust is very troublesome. We have a good share of ants about, and any quantity of fleas and mosquitoes. The mosquitoes are the most cruel of all.

Feb 5th Weather warm. Got a little gold today.

Feb 8th We raised about 8 divots of gold today. Weather hot.

Feb 10th Saturday. Weather as usual. Afternoon we went to Castlemaine, where we sold our gold, for which we got £5"1"0.
We heard of a party of four have found a piece of gold, about 22lb weight, worth about £1000 Sterling. The party who found it are spreeing[7] it away as fast as possible.

Feb 11th Sunday. A fine cool breeze, which is a treat. We are mainly employed in writing, and enjoying the fine breeze, which is very refreshing after a week of very hot weather.

---

[7] spending and general overindulgence.

Feb 17th We have done middling this week, having earned 2 ounces, 9 penney weight, for which we received £9"3"0 at the rate of £3"4"9 per ounce.

I sent a newspaper for the hall, and sent a letter home, and one to some shipmates at Ballarat.

Feb 18th Sunday afternoon. We had a stroll in the woods, which was very pleasant.

Feb 21st We bought an English newspaper, for 1s"6p. The name of it was Lloyds Weekly London Newspaper. This English news is very interesting.

Feb 24th Weather warm. We put up a rough table in our tent.

Feb 25th Sunday. We did little else but rest and read, as the weather is too hot for walking.

Mar 3rd We have good wages this week. We did not sell our gold this week.

March 5th My chest has arrived here from Melbourne, at which place I left it when we set off for the diggings. The carriage for cost 20 shillings.

March 7th I bought the few tools which I sold, on first starting to dig.

March 8th Weather warm. Bought some wood, and commenced to make a barrow. The wood cost £1"1"0.

March 10th We sold our gold which we had earned in the week. We received £26"8"0.
Our vituals cost us only 20 shillings each this week, but we have got very plain fare.

March 25th Our claim worked out. We heard tell of some new diggings been found out, a few miles farther up the country, so we set off to try and find them out and see for ourselves.
We had our bedding and some bread, and the like, beside a pot to boil tea or coffee in, as we expected to be a day or two away. We did not get far till we missed the track. After this we made the best of our way to the nearest dwelling to make enquiries respecting the road. The directions we got, took a long way back on the same road we had gone. However, we trudged on till daylight began to leave, so we agreed to pitch our quarters beside a small stream near at hand. We soon had a fire lit and some tea made. This we enjoyed very much, as we were both tired and hungry.
We rigged a tent out of part of our bedding and some bushes. In this rough and ready bed we slept, not very soundly, till morning.

March 26th We rose early and had some breakfast. After which we packed up and off again. The country, about this neighbourhood, is very fine. We tramped on for a good distance. At last we arrived at the long expected. This was a sight which might not be soon forget.

We entered by a narrow gorge, which opened out into a large park like ground, occupied by a large number of tents straggling about among the thick, bushy underwood and lofty trees, many of which the diggers were felling to make windlasses and the like.

We had a look round among the diggings. The wonderful accounts, which we heard at a distance, are now very poor when we get them from men that have tried the place.

We saw two or three people we know. They gave us a very poor account, so we thought the best plan would be to get back to the old spot as soon as possible.

We started next day, in a dray, for Campbells Creek. We paid 10s each for our ride. The dray man did not know the road. We went over twice the ground in consequence. In passing along the road we saw three emus, an Australian Ostrich.

We arrived at our tent, toward evening, quite satisfied with our journey.

We joined to another partner, and commenced to work on a hill in the neighbourhood.

March 31st We only earned 16 divots of gold this week, among three of us.

April 7th We have done a little better this week. We have earned £2"5"0, among the three, but this would not pay, so we separated from our new mate.

April 11th Got our tent removed to the opposite side of the main road. We pitched on a hill side, which is more healthy and pleasant than the flats, which were little else but swamps in wet weather.

April 12th We started to sink a hole in a place named Poverty Gulley. Weather very cool this morning. There was a strong, white frost upon the ground. The water in our bucket was frozen.

April 14th Sent a letter home.

April 17th We bought half a load of potatoes for 19 shilling, being at the rate of 4 pence per lb. We paid 6 per lb, retail price.

April 21st We got to the bottom of the hole, in Poverty Gully. It had no gold in it, so we gave it up as a bad job. It was 26 feet deep. We were 9 days in sinking it.
We tried a good many old holes in other gullys, but to no purpose.

April 23rd Started again to work on Campbells Flat. The ground is a little wet.

April 25th We had a walk to Fryers Creek to see our

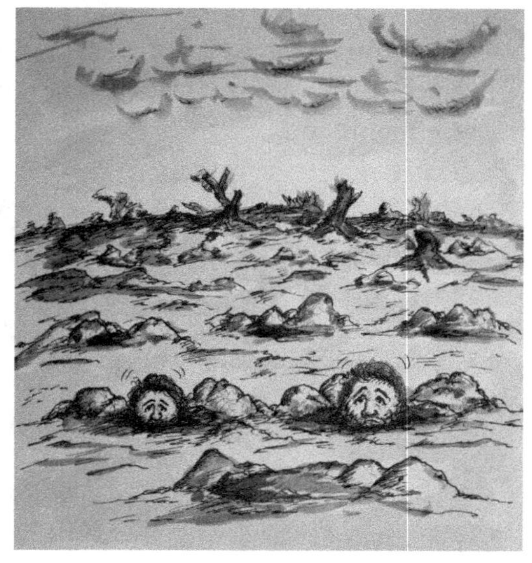

former mates, with whom we had our dinner and tea. They were very kind to us.

April 26th We went into another hole, which was only poor, averaging only half penny weight to the tub.

April 30th . We sold our gold, for which we received £2"1'0, at the rate of £3"13"0 per ounce. Weather cold and damp.

May 1st Weather very wet and cold.

May 2nd Weather milder. Wind from north coast.

May 3rd We left the flat and started to work our Forty Feet Hill again.

May 4th Weather fine.
In the afternoon I helped to carry a neighbour's child to the cemetery. There was no priest in attendance. One of the party had to read the service.
Bread at present selling at 3s"6p per four pound loaf.

May 12th We sold the produce of our labour for £13"76"6", at the rate of £3"14"8 per ounce.

May 14th We bought a newspaper. It contained the news of the death of the Emperor of Russia.
The price of bread reduced to 3s the 4 pound loaf.

May 19th We sold our gold for £14"16"0, at the rate of £3"14"0 per ounce.

May 22nd I bought a pair of water tight boots for 17s. They were English made.

May 23rd Weather very cold this morning.

May 28th We started to build a chimney at the end of our tent. Sent a newspaper to England.

May 30th Got our chimney completed. It makes the tent very comfortable when the fire is lit.

June 3rd Weather fine. The country looks well, after the late wet weather.

June 10th Wrote a letter for home.

June 12th We sold our gold for which we received £23"8"0, at the rate of £3"16"0 per ounce.

June 15th Weather fine and mild.

June 16th We had a walk to Castlemaine, this afternoon, where we saw one of our fellow passengers. Him and his mate were busy putting up a store for themselves. They had made a little money by chaff cutting at a farm, a short distance from Melbourne.
Weather fine. Things very brisk in Castlemaine.

June 17th Weather fine, but very cold first thing in the morning, but not so cold as in England, as thin walls of cotton would not shelter us.

June 21st Weather very fine. George posted a letter to his brother, Jonathan. Today is the shortest here. The sun rises at half past seven, and sets at half past four.

June 23rd. Weather fine and clear. This is the finest weather we have had since we arrived in the colony. We have earned 6 ounce since we sold the last gold. In the afternoon we had a walk to Castlemaine, where we posted a newspaper for home. It was named The Mount Alexander Mail, date June 22, 1855.

June 24th Weather fine. Our claim is nearly worked out. We had a walk to Barkers Creek, where there is a rush at present, which is expected to turn out well.
It is distant about 5 miles from our place.
There is some very good scenery along the road to it.

June 25th We rose early and went of to the rush on Barkers Creek. We sunk one hole. It was five feet deep, but we got nothing out of it. We tried a few holes that were already sunk. None of them were any use.

Some parties doing well on this ground. We returned to our tent well tired with our days work.

June 26th We agreed to give the new place a good trial. I took my swag (which consisted of bedding and a few provisions) and went off. George stopped at the old spot, to try and get as much gold out of the old claim as would clear expenses.

I worked till night, but to no account.

There were some acquaintances of ours working here. They had a tent with them, so I lodged in it.

June 30th Weather very clear and cool. At night the moon shone very clear. We could see to read a newspaper distinctly. The paper contained the news of the arrival of the mail ship Marco Polo, with English news up to the 6th of April, on which day she left Liverpool. She arrived here on the 29th of June.

I tried a tub full of surface gravel to see if there was any gold in it, as there were some good surface claims in the neighbourhood.

Afternoon I set off for our old smid, on Campbells Creek. This place was almost like a home, as we had never been tented anywhere else.

Gold at the above date selling at £3"18"0.

July 1st Weather dull and wet, but not cold.

July 2nd Weather very damp. We went down an old hole, to see if we could raise as much gold as would buy vituals, but we did not get any.

July 7th Weather showery. In the afternoon we got a stock of fire wood to our tent. After this we went to Castlemaine where we sold the gold which we had saved since selling the last. We received £23"16"0, at the rate of £3"16"0 per ounce. I deposited £20 in the Bank of New South Wales, to be remitted home. It cost 10 shillings to send it.

After arriving at our tent there was a heavy shower of hail, with thunder and lightning.

July 8th Weather wet. Wrote a letter for home.

July 9th Weather dull. A few light showers fell through the day. I helped our neighbour, Simpson, to take his frame tent down, as he intended to remove to Barkers Creek.

July 12th We sank a hole on a hill near Fourty Feet Hill. We only got a quarter of a penny weight off the bottom, so we gave it up and went off and had a try among the old holes, which some time turn out very well.

July 13th We went down an old hole. We saw a little gold, so we commenced to drive down some wash stuff.

July 14th George went down another old hole, about 30 yards from the one we went down yesterday. We intended to drive towards each other, along the west side of the reef, which is generally composed of slate and pipeclay. We got very little gold out of this old claim.

July 15th Weather dull and cold. We were mainly employed in cooking, eating and writing. Very dull for want of company.

July 19th We sold the little gold we had got for which we received £2"7"0, at the rate of £3"10"0

July 20th We had a stroll round among the old holes in the neighbourhood to see if there was any chance of finding a payable claim. We went down a few holes on Seventy Feet Hill.
These holes were very awkward to get up and down, as the feet holds were in many places broken away. We intended to work a few of them, so we took a windlass, and rope, and commenced to work one.

July 21st Weather dull. We drove a lot of wash stuff out, but we saw no gold in it.
This afternoon George posted a newspaper to his mother. The name of the paper was The Melbourne Weekly Herald.

July 22nd Weather very windy and cold. We had a visit from one of our Fryers Creek friends. One of their party is sick of colonial fever. This disease takes great hold of Europeans.

Pig problems

July 23rd Weather rather milder today.

At night when we got to our tent, the pigs had been in, and destroyed ever so much bread, candles and flour, besides turning every moveable thing upside down. This was not the first time they had paid us a visit. These swine are a great trouble to the diggers in the neighbourhood of their rambles.

July 28th Weather fine. We had a walk to Castlemaine, where we sold our gold for which we received £2"6"6. The rate per ounce £3"16"0. I posted a paper for brother George. It was named The Melbourne Daily Age.

July 24 There was a large number of persons at the Post Office, enquiring for letters and newspapers from home and friends.

July 29th Weather pleasant for walking. After breakfast we took a stroll as far as Barker Creek, to see our old neighbour Simpson. Him and his mate had only done very little good, since moving to Barker Creek.

There seems a prospect of this district turning out well, as there are many parties trying the ground. What gold is found here is generally lying in patches, so that some parties got a good prize, while the majority got nothing.

There is great talk of a great rush at present, to a place named Kangaroo Hill, which is about 5 miles from our tent, in a southerly direction. The sinking is very hard and deep. There are several feet of ironstone to go through. The depth of the holes is 80 feet. These holes cannot be put down without a little capital.

July 30th Weather damp and cold. At night the rain fell plentifully.

Aug 1st Today we washed two loads of gravel, which we got out of the hole on Seventy Feet Hill. From this gravel we got only half an ounce. This quantity would not pay to work old, deep ground, so we gave it up.

Aug 2nd Weather mild. After breakfast we had a look around among some more claims, to see if we could find a payable place to dig in, but the ground in this neighbourhood is nearly all worked out.

In the afternoon we had a stroll to Barkers Creek, to see if it should be advisable to shift our tent to that place, but the accounts we heard gave us very little prospect to shift our tent, so we gave up the notion.

There are two or three parties doing some good here, but the majority are doing very poor. Campbell Creek is nearly deserted, at present, owing to so many rushes in the neighbouring districts.

George posted a newspaper for his brother Jonathan. It was the Melbourne Daily Age, dated July 31.

The ship, Oliver Lang, arrived in Port Phillip after a passage of ninety days. She brought a mail. We had later news by a ship, which arrived before her. She belonged to the White Star Line of packets.

Aug 3rd We had another look about, to seek a place to set in. We saw an acquaintance busy. He said he was doing middling. He advised us to sink a hole next to him, so we marked a claim out, ready for starting with next day.

The name of the place was Slaty Gully, about a mile from our tent.

Aug 4th We commenced to sink. We sunk down about 6 feet by 12 o'clock, when we left of work for the day. Been Saturday afternoon, we went to Castlemaine, where the diggers were electing persons to form a local court, to award justice in cases of dispute in digging operations.

We sold our gold for £1"18"0, at the rate of £3"16"0 per ounce.

We purchased a few groceries, and some writing paper, envelopes and a Lloyds Weekly London Newspaper, dated May 6th, 1855.

We get to the tent, when nearly dark, after very awkward navigation among muddy roads.

Aug 5th Sunday. Weather dull. We are mainly employed in writing, and reading the newspaper. This helps to pass the time away, which should be otherwise burdensome.

Aug 6th Weather as usual. We got to the bottom of our claim in Slaty Gully. The hole was no good, so we gave it up.

We had a fine sight when we arrived at the tent.

The pigs were in.

They had burst right through the end and eaten everything that was eatable, beside turning the place upside down. They pulled my bedclothes off and, rolling in them, making them in a horrid state.

We went to the parties who the swine belonged to, to see if we could get any compensation, but they would not give any satisfaction, so we got a

summons for them to appear at the Court of Castlemaine.
We laid the damages at £3"0"0.
This was the fifth time the pigs had been in our tent, and destroyed things.

Aug 7th We commenced to sink a hole on Campbells Flat. There were a good many parties busy. Some had got to the bottom, which was hardly workable without pumps, as the water came in so fast.

Aug 8th George went to appear against the owner of the pigs, but the case could not be settled as there was no witnesses up, to prove that the pigs belonged to the owner, but the magistrate said that he was liable to a fine of ten pounds for having his swine running loose on the roads.
The owner did not deny that his (swine) ran loose. The

magistrate advised him to make it up with us, so at night the owner came up to our tent, and settled with us. We took £2"10"0, and finished the dispute.

Aug 10th Weather fine. We rued sinking the hole on the flat, as a good many parties had left, owing to their claims been too wet to work.

We next steered our course to a hill in the neighbourhood, on which a good many parties were sinking on.

After looking round a while, we agreed to sink a hole which was partly down. This was rather wet, owing to water oozing in at the sides.

Aug 11th Wind cool. We expect to get to the bottom of our shaft by Monday. In the afternoon we got a stock of fire wood in.

Aug 12th Sunday. Weather very fine. We had a visit from one of our Fryers Creek friends, as he was on his way to Castlemaine Primitive Methodist Chapel, at which place he was going to preach.

Aug 13th We got to the bottom of our shaft by 12 o'clock in the afternoon We tried six tub full's of stuff, from which we got six divots of gold. We were satisfied with this prospect.

Aug 14th Weather fine. This morning we scraped the bottom of our shaft, from them we got 2 ½ Ounces of gold. The driving in the hole next to us is very hard, so that they can only drive about 2 feet per day.

Aug 16th Weather quite changed. It has been raining heavy all last night, accompanied by heavy claps of thunder, which were not very good for lulling to sleep when tormented with toothache, as I was.

This morning the creek was very much swelling, and the water was rushing along with great force, so that the only bridge (within a mile or two) was swept away. We had to travel about 3 miles to get to our work.

When we got there, our pit had a great quantity of water in it. We got the water out, as soon as possible, and scraped some more of the bottom up. From this we got about 3 ½ ounce. We left work at 2 o'clock.

As we were wet, when we got to our tent, we were rather tired. In the evening we bought a pair of small scales, for 15 shillings, for weighing our gold with. We had got out of our new claim 6 ½ ounces.

Aug 17th Weather fine. We commenced to sink a shaft, at the far end of our claim, to prevent the parties next to us from taking our ground, which is very often the case. The water oozes in at the sides.

We bought a newspaper named the Melbourne Weekly Herald, for which we paid 2 shillings.

In the afternoon we got a stock of firewood in, after which we went to Castlemaine, where I posted a newspaper for home.

There were some horses sold very cheap at the sale yards.

Aug 19th Weather as usual. I wrote a letter for home. Rather a hard job when news are scarce.

Aug 20th I posted a letter and registered it.

Today we got to the bottom of our new shaft, but it was not much worth. We only got a few penny weights off the bottom. Our next neighbours had taken part of our ground before we got down.

Aug 23rd Weather dull. We got 1½ ounces today.

Aug 24th Weather stormy and wet.
It is a year, to day, since we left home.

Aug 25th Today we got 2 ounces"15 of gold. In the afternoon got some wood, and repaired our cradle.

Aug 26th The wind blew very hard through last night. It is not quite so windy this morning, but the weather is very wet and cold. The wind is from the south west.

Aug 30th We got 1½ ounce to day. We bought a Lloyds Weekly London newspaper, for 1s"6p.

Aug 31st We got a ¼ ounce today.

Sept 1st Weather dull, but not cold. We had a dispute with the men in the next claim to us. They had taken ever so much of our ground, so we got some disinterested parties to arbitrate between us. The result was that we had to have 2 loads of washing stuff, as damages.

Sept 2nd Weather mild today, Sunday. There are a good many mice flitting about the tent. They are very destructive to the vituals. After dinner we had a ramble in search of wild flowers We gathered a good many different kinds. Among them was the Sarsaparilla, which is used for medicinal purposes. The flower is a lilac colour. The others were all fine flowers, some of which might have graced any English garden.

We arrived at our tent at about 5 O'clock, with the reward of our labour in the shape of a bunch of flowers.

Sept 3rd We washed the load of stuff we got for damages. We got 9 wts of gold out of it. In the afternoon we commenced to drift around our claim, so as to prevent any one taking any more of our ground. The weather fine.

Sept 5th We washed 1½ ounce from 6 buckets of stuff of gravel.

Sept 8th Weather fine. We have earned 5 ounces of gold this week. A year today, from Liverpool.

George's box arrived from Melbourne.

Sept 9th Weather very pleasant. We got dinner early and went of for a walk to Barkers Creek, to see our old

neighbour, Simpson. The scenery along the road was beautiful, with the wattle trees been in blossom, which is a fine orange yellow. They scent the air with an odour much resembling that of the hawthorn blossom.

There has been a good many stores put up along the road, since the rush first took place. There are a few people doing very well on these diggings, but the majority are just making a living. But our friend, Simpson, has had very bad luck. He has been off work for three weeks with a sore finger.

It was bit by a scorpion, while he was cleaning out the decayed trunk of a an old tree before setting it on fire. If he had been bit in the summertime, instead of the Spring, the bite would have been fatal. They are torpid in the cold weather.

Our friend keeps up his spirits, in the hope that someday he will get back to the Cape of Good Hope colony, at which he had been for a good number of years.

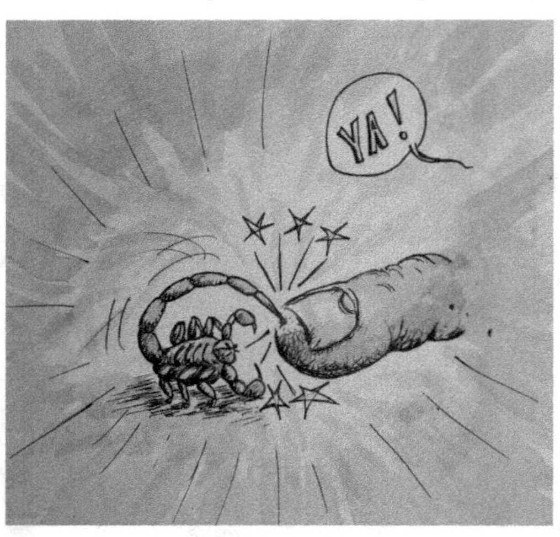

He was mainly employed in trading with the natives of the Interior, but when on his last expedition, he was plundered to the amount of twelve hundred pounds Sterling, in articles which he had purchased from the natives. He blamed a missionary as been the cause of the robbers.

While we were rambling about the bush we saw the nest of an Australian lennet. The nest had two eggs in it. They are the same colour as the English Hedge Sparrow. They are stripped with brown. The nest is a very rough affair, been made of twigs and leaves alone without any soft lining of moss or feather as is mostly the case with our English small birds.

We set off for home, at 3 o'clock, and arrived a 5 in good order for tea, which we soon made ready.

Sept 14th Weather as usual. We got 6 ounces of gold this afternoon. This is the best days work we have had yet.

Castlemaine gymnastics

Sept 15th We got 1 ounce"16dwts", today. Afternoon we went to Castlemaine. I posted a letter enquiring of the Postmaster about a letter I saw addressed for me, in the unclaimed letter list. We sold 1 ounce"6dwts" of gold, for which we got £4"15"0, been at the rate of £3"15"9 per ounce.
There was a great deal of stir, in the main square of Castlemaine, owing to some Americans performing in gymnastics. They had a rope about 300 feet long, stretched from the stump of an old tree to the top of another tree, which was about 60 feet high.

Up this rope a female had to walk, without any support but a long pole to balance her body. Beside this feat there were some wonderful performances to be gone through on the slack rope, which was erected in front of the largest hotel in Castlemaine. There was a large baboon, or ape, set upon a ladder in front of the hotel. He was kept hard at work cracking nuts and eating apples, oranges and different kinds of sweet meats, which were thrown from the crowd which was collected in front, enjoying the fun.

Sept 16th Sunday. Weather fine. George had a walk to fryers Creeks to see our mates.

Sept 17th Weather rather stormy. We washed out 1 ounce"15dwts", to day. There are some holes about us that are not paying.

Sept 18th We washed 6 loads of stuff in a long tom[8]. We got 2 ounce"14dwts, from it.

George sick again

Sept 20th Weather dull. We washed 2 ounces "2½dwts" out, to day. George taken ill again, with dysentery, in the evening. He took some cayenne pepper and brandy. This did no good.

---

[8] A long tom was a long wooden wash box with a screen at the end used to separate large rocks from a load, and to allow gold to wash to a lower level.

Sept 21st George very weak. He took some castor oil, which caused him to vomit a little.

Sept 22nd Weather cold. George very ill. A woman in the next tent made some arrow root for him. This seemed to do him a little good.

Sept 24th Weather dull and wet. George a little better today. I received a letter from home.

Sept 25th George is still improving.

Sept 26th I altered our chimney as it did not draw freely.

Sept 30th Weather dull. We got some fire wood to our tent. We commenced to board at Mrs. Brewers. At night there was a heavy thunder storm. The lightning was very strong. It illuminated the county for many miles around.

Oct 3rd George started work today.

Oct 5th Weather fine. George commenced to sink a new claim in the gully, while I finished the old claim.

Oct 7th Weather as usual. We have earned 1 ounce"9½ dwts[9] this week. We sold it for £5"7"0. While we were at Castlemaine we were in the public auction house, where there was women's shoes sold for 12s per dozen pairs.

---

[9] dwts is an abbreviation of a pennyweight (about 1.556 grams)

Oct 9th We gave the old claim up as it was worked out. We washed five loads of stuff out, in the long tom. We got 2 ounce"13 dwts of gold from it.

Oct 12th We got to the bottom of our new shaft. There was a little gold in it.

Oct 14th We sold 2 ounces" 14 dwts, at £3"15'0 per ounce.

Oct 16th Weather showery to day. We washed 5 loads of stuff, from which we got 1 ounce"1 dwts of gold.

Oct 21st We received a letter from our friends of the hall. It was dated May 27th, so it has been 5 months coming to hand.
We sold 2 ounces, 18dwts of gold, for which we got £11"0"0 at £3"15"0 per ounce.

Oct 22nd Weather very fine. One of our former mates, from Fryers Creek, to see us. He came on horseback. At night we went so far on the road with him, George and I each had a ride on his horse. This was the first time either of us had been on horseback.

Oct 23ʳᵈ Weather fine. We sent £30 to…(left blank by the writer). In the afternoon we washed two loads of stuff, from which we got 1ounce"7dwts of gold.

Oct 26ᵗʰ There was a heavy thunder storm, and much rain. It fell in torrents for a short time. The lightning, which was very heavy, struck an old tree in the neighbourhood of our tent. The tree was split to atoms. After the storm had subsided a little, we commenced to wash some stuff in the long tom. We got 7 ounce"7"0" from it.

Oct 27ᵗʰ Weather fine and cool after the storm.

Oct 28ᵗʰ We sold our gold for £9"11"0 at £3"15"0 per ounce. We bought an English newspaper. It was dated Aug 5, 1855.

Oct 31ˢᵗ We commenced to sink another shaft, as the one we are in is nearly worked out. There is a rush on the other side of the creek. It is reported that some parties are working two ounces to the tub..

Nov 1ˢᵗ We washed five loads of stuff, from which we got 2 ounces"3wts"0

Nov 2ⁿᵈ Weather showery. We could not sink the shaft any farther, as the water came in through the sides of the shaft.

Nov 3rd Weather fine. We had a stroll to Castlemaine, in the afternoon, where we sold the gold we got from the five loads. We got £7"11"0 at £3"15"0 per ounce.
We called at the post office. There was a great number, some wanting letters and some newspapers.

Nov 5th Weather warm. Summer is taking possession of the county, once more. The ground is very warm.

Nov 6th We washed two tubs full of stuff, from which we got one penny weight and half.

Nov 7th Weather hot. We washed 3 tubs, from which we got 2½ dwts. This would not pay for working the claim, so we gave it up and commenced to sink another hole.

Nov 8th Weather dull. Finished the sinking of the hole, which turned out no good. We sank other two holes, six feet each. They were no use.

Nov 9th Weather fine. This morning we took a stroll among the diggings, to see if there was any chance of getting a good claim. We saw a quartz reef, near Poverty Gully. Some parties were doing a little good. In the afternoon we had a stroll in another direction, where we started to sink a hole near some old working.
At night the weather stormy.

Nov 10th Weather very stormy, over night. There has been many an old tent striped of its coverings, while many were levelled with the ground.

We got the bottom of the shaft. There was a few small specks of gold in it, but not as much as would pay for working it. Today is the nomination of the candidates for the council. The names of the parties were Pike, Palmer and Wheeler. The show of hands were in favour of the first two. After the nomination, Pike and Palmer took a drive round the township, followed by a great many diggers and others interested in the proceedings.

Nov 11th Weather dull and cold. In the evening our friend Simpson paid us a visit, his finger was better, and he had started work and had done very well, so far since.

Nov 12th We commenced to sink, to try and get the quartz reef. The shaft is about 7 feet long by 3 feet wide. We sank about 5 feet today.

Nov 13th The sinking is harder, as we get farther down. We set our windlass over the shaft.

Nov 14th This afternoon we went to see the proceedings at the polling booths. There was a great many quarrels between the rival parties. One of the mob taken into custody, for using a knife too freely among the crowd.

The contest between the candidates was very hard.

At 4 o'clock, the returning officer declared the state of the poll. The candidates returned were Pike and Wheeler, Palmer been rejected as been connected with the squatting interests.

Nov 17th Damp and cold.

Nov 20th Weather very warm and sultry. We have got to the surface of the quartz reef. We broke about a foot into the reef, but there was no signs of gold. In the afternoon we bought an English newspaper, bought out be the royal mail ship Emma.

Nov 21st Weather still warm. Vegetation is assuming a brown appearance, as the heat becomes more intense.

Nov 26th We washed our blankets this afternoon. At night we had a heavy thunder storm.

Nov 28th Weather warm. George commenced to sink a shaft, on a hill in the neighbourhood of Fourty Feet Hill, while I tried the reef a little longer.

Nov 29th Weather hot. At night the bull frogs croaking very much.

Killer elephant

Nov 30th Weather very hot. In the evening we saw an elephant taken along the road, in the custody of police. It is reported that it had killed a man, near the Jim Crow Rangers.
We gave up the reef.
We bought a newspaper, bought out by the mail ship, Lightning.

Today we both started to work on the hard hill, a shaft which was nearly bottomed. We tried with the pick, but the stuff was too hard.

Dec 1st We commenced to blast the hole, but it did no good. Weather warm.

Dec 2nd Sunday we had a walk afternoon.

Dec 3rd Our shaft is over hard to work, with either blasting or gads[10]. We put two shots in, and fired them, but they took no effect. After dinner we commenced to sink a hole at a rush, on a hill opposite, known as Stoughton House Hill.
One or two parties had got gold to pay.

Dec 7th Weather very hot. We are 27 feet down, with our shaft, but no signs of gold yet. We bought a Lloyds newspaper, dated Sep 16th, 1855.

---

[10] a sharp spike of metal, hit with a large hammer.

Dec 8th Weather scorching hot. Wind from the north. The dust is flying along in dense clouds.

Dec 9th We commenced to sink another hole, as the one we sank last had no gold in it. We got as near as possible to a party, who were getting what paid them.

Dec 11th There has been a heavy fall of rain in the night. Today very cloudy.

Dec 14th Weather very hot. We got to the bottom of our shaft, which was no better than the last. The depth was 26 feet. We drove about 3 feet in, but no sign of gold.

Dec 15th We shifted our windlass over the hole next to ours. It was sunk by some Cornish men. They got a little gold from it, but not so much as to pay for working it.
Today we discontinued boarding at Mrs. Brewers, as circumstance did not suit to stop any longer.
Gold is very scarce with us at present.
We have got none for seven weeks past. Today we bought an American axe for 16 shillings. They are used to chop fire wood with.

Dec 16th Weather very close. We went to a large water hole and had a bath, which refreshed us very much.

Dec 17th Weather sultry. We got a small quantity of gold out of the hole, so we continued to drive. In the afternoon a heavy thunderstorm, and plenty of rain.

Dec 18th We got 2 dwts of gold today. At night there was a very heavy thunderstorm. Just before the storm came on there was a dead calm but, when the storm came, it commenced in good earnest. The sky was illumined for a few minutes together. The country, for miles around, was as plainly seen as tho the Sun had been shining. The lightning reflected various colours, along the clouds. The

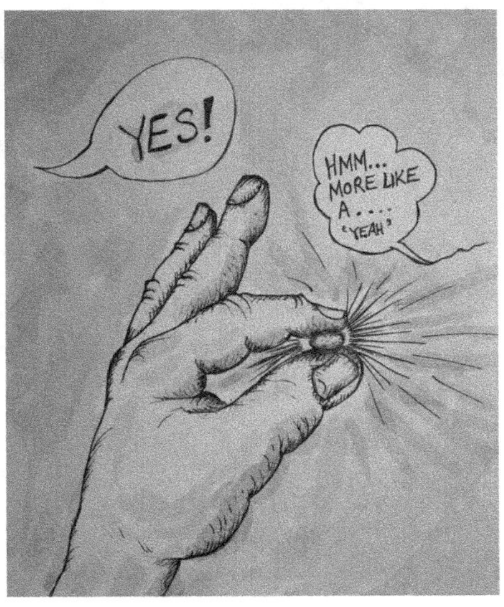

rain fell very fast for half an hour and, in that short time, the creek or stream had rose about 3 feet.

At 8 o'clock the moon shone out, as calmly as tho no storm had been raging.

Dec 19th Weather pleasant after the storm. We fell in with a little patch of gold. There was about 6 ounces of it. This raised our spirits a little.

Dec 21st Today we got 2½ ounces. This is the longest day in the Southern Hemisphere. Sun rises at half past four, and sets at half past seven o'clock.

This is the anniversary of our arrival in the colony of Victoria.

We decorated our tent inside, with the engravings from the Illustrated London News.

Dec 24th We got 1 ounce"4 dwts today. There are some sports going on, not far from our place.

Dec 25th Weather warm today, Christmas. We had a plumb pudding for dinner, but the weather is too warm to relish old English fare.

Dec 27th We washed 2 loads of stuff, from which we got 1½ ounces. There is very little wash stuff in the drift we are working at present. The gold we do get, in this drive, is mainly on the bottom.

Dec 28th We got 8 dwts today.

Dec 29th Weather wet, so we did not commence work.

Dec 30th Weather warm. We got about 5 ounces of gold today. This will help to make up for past ill luck.

Jan 1st 1856 Weather very hot. Not a cloud to be seen all day. There were races to take place at a short distance from Campbells Creek. There were a good many people

going along the road, toward the races. Some were on horseback, and others different kinds of conveyances. George set off to walk as far. He did not go far till he turned back, as the heat was too much to hide out a shelter.

Jan 2nd Weather hot. Not the least breath of air stirring. We got a little gold today.

Jan 3rd Weather hot as usual. The air very bad down the shaft. The candle burnt, but dimly. It sometimes died out. It is against the health working, when the air is so close.

Jan 4th. We got a little gold to day.

Jan 5th Weather fine. A cool breeze from the south. We washed one load of stuff, from which we got 27 dwts. We have earned 11¾ this week.

Jan 12th We got 8 ounces. In the afternoon we walk to Castlemaine. I posted a letter for home. We bought a newspaper. There is a good supply of vegetables in the market.

Jan 13th Weather fine. Afternoon we took a stroll to Barkers Creek, to see our old neighbour Simpson. Him and his mate are doing very little at present.

Jan 19th We have got 2 ounces"5 dwts this week.

Jan 26th Weather excessively hot. There is no way of escape. We got 1 ounce"17dwts to day.

At night the mosquitoes are very troublesome. We hear there is likely to be war with America. The price of vegetables are very low at present. We buy potatoes, for 3½ per lb, while we paid 6 per lb when we first arrived here. Our living cost about 30 shilling per week.

Jan 31st We washed two loads of stuff, which gave us 1 ounce"10dwts of gold.

Feb 1st Weather fine. Today one of our neighbours (a butcher) was killed while riding on horseback. He came in contact with a tree when the horse was going very quick.

We have earned 3 ounce7dwts of gold. We bought an English paper, dated Nov 5th.

Feb 4th Weather very hot. We got 7 dwts to day. There is no sleeping in bed with bed cloths on.

Feb 5th We have got 4 ounces 10dwts of gold today. In the evening we had a thunderstorm with heavy rain, after which the air was cooler.

Feb 6th Damp. We got 5 dwts of gold. At night another thunderstorm, with rain.

Feb 7th Weather close and wet, it has been rainy all last night. We had to give over working down the hole this afternoon, as the candles would not burn, owing to the air been foul. George is repairing the wind sail, so as to cause a better draft. Our tent bottom is very damp, as the water oozes in at the sides and end.

Feb 8th Weather very wet. The rain has been falling fast all night. There is

a heavy flood today. The creek having over flown its banks, and the adjoining flats. There are plenty of tubs and cradles drifting down with the stream. There are heavy logs of timber washed right onto the main road.

All bridges (such as they were) are washed away.

Feb 9th Weather moderate. When we got to our claim, the workings were nearly all filled up with water and mud. We managed to get our tools out. Today, George got a letter from his brother, Jonathan. It was dated Nov 1, 1855.

At night, one of our Fryers Creek friends called to see us. He had been to Castlemaine sale yards, selling a cart. We went along the road with him a mile, or two. There puddling machine is paying very poor at present.

Feb 11th Weather fine. We commenced to sink another shaft to try and get into the old claim where we left off.

Feb 15th We got to the bottom of the shaft, which came right upon the end of the old drift. There is a good deal of water to bail out, before we can work the ground.

Feb 16th Very hot. Afternoon we went to Castlemaine, where there was a meeting called to elect proper persons to form a local court. The promise of which is to look after the digging interests. The majority of diggers were opposed to the election, till the present Chairman was dismissed. He been a Government man, and opposed to a flat piece of ground (in front of the Government Camp) been used for digging purposes.

I received a letter from home. It was dated Nov 2nd 1855. We got an English Newspaper, dated Nov 18th 1855.

There is a good display of fruit in the market. Fruit is selling at from 9s to 1s"6p per lb. Gold is selling at £3"13"6 per ounce.

We work one load of stuff, which gave us 1ounce"12dwts of gold.

Feb 17th Weather very hot. Too hot for walking, so we passed the day in reading, and writing. I wrote a letter to William Routledge.

Feb 23rd Weather very hot in the afternoon. We got 5 ounces this week.

Feb 28th Weather still very hot, through the day, but very cold in the night.

March 1st We have earned 22 ounces this week. In the afternoon I posted a letter for home. I enquired for a letter from William Routledge, but there was none.

March 8th Weather warm. We have got 9 ounces this week. The ground is very hard to work. It soon blunts the picks.

March 9th Very hot. The little wind there is, is from the north, bringing with it the hot blast from the tropics. The ink dries as fast as it is laid on the paper. There is talk of calling in the aid of capitalists, in working old ground and quality reefs, as it is almost impossible to work some places without a combination of labour and capital.

March 15th Weather wet through last night. Today very warm. We have got 10ounce 13dwts this week.

We went to Castlemaine, where there was a monster meeting called to consider the proprietary of digging on the camp ground, in opposition to the authorities. After two or three speakers had done, the whole meeting went to the camp ground. Most of the diggers commenced to work claims out.

One person started to dig. He was soon taken into custody.

Some of the diggers were very rough with the police. This nearly ended in a riot. The man was soon bailed out by a committee, which was formed to enquire into the lawfulness of digging for gold on the camp ground.

At night rain and lightning.

There are too many mice in our tent at present.

March 22nd Weather damp. We have got 2 ounce this week.

March 23rd Easter Sunday. We have got our chimney mended up for the winter.

March 25th We washed 4 loads of

stuff, from which we got 4 ounce 7 dwts of gold, beside 1ounce"2 dwts, which we scraped of the bottom of the drive.

March 27th Weather stormy. We had a very heavy thunderstorm through last night. Today the Marco Polo ship sailed, with the mail for England.

March 29th I sold 25ounce"18 dwts of gold, for which I received £101"7"6 at £3"18"3 per ounce. This was the highest price we have ever received. We saw two of our old mates from Fryers Creek. They were trying to sell two of their horses, and intended to buy another. They are doing muddling with the puddling machine.

March 30th Weather close and dull. We hear that a person named Golightly is going home to Monkwean Nouth[11].
We intend to see him before he sails.

April 3rd Dull. We washed 4 loads of stuff in the long tom. We got 10 ounces of gold from it

April 5th Weather wet. We did not start work today. We saw Mr. Golightly. He promised to take a letter home for us. This afternoon we bought a Lloyds Weekly London newspaper, containing news to the 16 of Dec.
There was an almost total eclipse of the sun this afternoon. It commenced at 3 o'clock and finished at 5 o'clock.

April 6th One of our fellow passengers called to see us. He was employed at Castlemaine at his own trade, which is tailor. He has very good wages.

April 7th Weather dull. We finished our claim this morning. Bought a newspaper from England, dated Jan 6th.

April 8th A fine cool breeze to day. We washed 1½ loads of stuff, from which we got 3ounces 7dwts of gold.

Lola Montez in Castlemaine

April 10th We had a walk as far as a place named Taylors Paddock, which was private property. The owner had given leave for the diggers

---

11 North eastern England, near Sunderland, County Durham.

to mine upon it, provided they paid 4 pounds each for claims which, if the diggers filled up when done with, would return one pound. A great many parties got nothing out of their claims.

At night we went to the Hall of Castlemaine, to see the celebrated Lola Montez[12]. We paid 7s"6p for admission to the back seats. The front seats were 10 shillings.

When she had concluded her performance, some person in the audience said something respecting her origin.

This sent her into a passion.

She said she did not care a half penny for any of the audience, for she had £70,000 of her own, and that they might think themselves highly honoured, that she had condescended to play before them.

---

[12] Lola Montez was a World wide celebrated performer of the time. Born Eliza Rosanna Gilbert, in Ireland, she assumed the stage name of Lola Montez, and became famous as the 'Spanish Dancer' and mistresses of King Ludwig 1 of Bavaria and Alexandre Dumas (to name a few). She toured all of Europe, Australia and the United States.

April 14th Weather fine. We had a walk as far as a hill, about 4 miles from our tent. The hill is of volcanic formation. There are two men sinking a shaft. It is a kind of lava. It is very hard to get through. They have been six weeks in sinking 40 feet. They expect to get to the bottom at 70 feet.

They wanted us to join them, so that two might work night shifts, and the other in the day time. We did not think there was any inducement, as there had been no gold been found near, or in, the neighbourhood.

April 15th I received a letter from home. It was dated Dec 16th, 1855.

April 16th We commenced to sink another shaft, near the one we were in last. In the evening we bought a newspaper, containing 40 days later news. It was bought out by the steam ship Royal Charter, of the Eagle Line of Packets.

She has made the passage from Plymouth in 59 days. This is the quickest passage on record. We bought news up the 16th February.

April 17th Weather very dull and wet. We got a stock of firewood in the morning.

April 18th Wet and cold.

April 19th Weather cold with, now and then, heavy showers or rain.

April 26th Weather very fine. Got a stock of fire wood in.

April 27th Cool and dull. We had a walk to Fryers Creek to see our old mates. They are only doing middling at present, with their puddling machine.
In our journey home at night, we missed the track and got straggling among the old working of some diggings.
We had great difficulty from falling into the many

holes of both mud and water, however we were lucky enough to find the right road in a short time. We arrived at our tent well tired with our journey.

April 28th Weather cold and stormy. We started to sink a hole on Fourty Feet Hill. After sinking 4 feet, we came to a hard crust, about 6 inches thick. It was very hard so that we had to use gads or steel wedge.

April 29th Dull. There are 3 feet more of crust, but not so hard as the first.

May 3rd Weather fine. We got to the bottom of the shaft. It was 18 feet deep. The rock at bottom is very unequal about this hill. There is one hole about 200 yards off ours. It is 80 feet deep. Afternoon we had a walk to Castlemaine, which place seems to be very thriving.

We saw some shares (in a steam mill company) for sale. It is expected to be a very payable concern for shareholders.
In the evening very warm.

May 4th In the afternoon we had a stroll into the bush as far as the Bald Hill, from which we had a splendid view of the surrounding country, which is densely wooded as far as the eye can reach. In

walking homeward, we saw a beautiful sunset. It reflected some beautiful colours on the distant ranges of hills.
We arrived at our tent at 6 o'clock.

May 5th Dull. We tried our shaft a little more, but to no purpose. Things are very dull on these diggings.

May 7th. Wet. Today, a Catholic priest tried in the police court of Castlemaine, for using threatening language and forcibly ejecting a reporter from the Catholic church of Castlemaine. The case was proved against the priest. He has to answer another charge (brought by a barrister at law), for slander.

May 9th Very wet and cold.

May 10th Weather very wind but not cold.

May 11th Fine. Things very slack here in the digging line of business. We have got no gold since April 8th.

May 12th Weather rather dull, but mild for the season, which is near mid winter. The following is a correct copy of some lines, which were posted upon a gum tree near Fryers Town, Colony of Victoria, Australia, on the 20th of April, 1856. Turn over:

To every one it may concern,

This is put up that ye may learn,
that scarcely any day goes by but some fowels
in the tent do fly of P.S Raphiel and his mate,
and ransack every dish and plate, each hole
and corner, pan and pot, pick every thing and mess
the lot, as we get neither egg nor chicken nor of
there bones have we the picking. This is the caution those
who own them, to keep them off, or else we'll stone them.

May 16th Commenced to sink a hole on the shallow part of 40 Feet Hill. Sinking rather soft.

May 17th Weather fine. I bought a blanket for 19 shillings. Bought a cap for 4 shillings.

May 18th Dull, and rather cold.

May 19th We are 14 feet deep, with our shaft today.

May 20th Weather very wet and cool.

May 21st Showers. We got to the bottom of our shaft, but it had no gold in it. In the evening commenced to write a letter.

May 22nd I posted a letter with (left blank by author)– enclosed, it cost £2 to send or remit the –(left blank by author)
I expect it to go by the mail ship Royal Charter, of the Eagle Line of Packets.

May 23rd Damp. We tried our claim a little more. We only got one fine speck of gold, so we gave it up. In the afternoon I started to make a little box, to hold pens and paper in.

May 24th Weather wet and cool. Finished the box making.

May 25th Today took an Emitc[13] as I did not feel well in the stomach.

May 26th Weather fine and clear in the morning. In the afternoon rather stormy. The Queen's birthday celebrated to day, instead of Saturday which was Marka Day[14].

Leaving the goldfields

May 27th Weather dull. This afternoon we bid farewell to the diggings. We started for Melbourne.
We engaged with a waggoneer to take us and our luggage. We pay two pounds each. In the evening we camped not far from Saw Pit Gully.
There was a batch of wagons there before us. The drivers had made a large fire on. We soon had tea cooked.
After tea was done, we sat around the fire listening to the drivers tell of their wonderful feats in their line of business. We made our bed inside the wagon, when we retired at 8 o'clock.

---

[13] Emitc was a stomach medicine of the time.
[14] Celebrating the beginning of the 8 hour work day.

May 28th Weather fine. We rose at 7 o'clock and got breakfast, after which we started on the road again. We travelled onto a place called 5 Miles Creek, at which place we camped for the night.

May 29th Weather dull. We commenced to go through the Black Forest, where the roads are very bad. Some places in the road the wheels were up to the nave in the mud. The horses stuck to their work bravely. After getting through the forest the roads were better, been macadamised[15].

May 30th We got to a place called The Gap, where we camped for the night. It was a fine natural meadow.

May 31st Weather fine. We arrived in Melbourne in the evening, at 4 o'clock. We put our boxes into a store, and went off in search of lodgings. We got our teas and lodgings for the night at a French boarding house. We paid 2 shillings each.

---

[15] A method of road building of the time, developed by Scottsman John McAdam. Layers of progressively large to small stones laid and crushed into the road to make an all weather surface.

June 1st Weather fine. We engaged a place to board and lodge to which place we removed our boxes.

We had to pay £1"8"0 each in advance for a weeks board and lodgings.

Melbourne is greatly enlarged since we left for the diggings in January 1855.

June 2nd Weather fine. We had a ramble through the city of Melbourne. Things are very dull at present. Today the Champion of the Seas arrived in Hobsons Bay with 300 passengers on board. She struck a sand bank at the heads, in coming in on Saturday.

June 3rd We saw one of our ship mates, named Henry Oats. He is about tired of Melbourne and would like to be from it as soon as possible, to some more likely place for his own trade, which is shipwright.

Departing Melbourne for home

June 10th Weather dull. On ship board, bound for London. Ship Kent, 1000 tons. We weighed anchor at 8 o'clock in the morning. We sailed down the bay to near Port Phillip Heads, where we dropped anchor for the day.

There is a vessel ahead of us bound for Liverpool. Her name is the Joseph Jarret, of the Black Ball Line of Packets. There is a bet between the Captain and our Captain, which will be home first.

June 11ᵗʰ Weather dull. Wind fair at noon. We weighed anchor and got under way to go though Port Phillip Heads. The ship, Joseph Jarret, about a mile ahead of us.

June 16ᵗʰ Weather dull. We are passing through Basses Straits [sic]. A good many small islands about us.

We sighted a small barque. She was supposed to be bound from Van Diemans land to Sydney.

June 17ᵗʰ Weather squally. Ship's flying jib boom carried away.

June 21ˢᵗ Weather moderate. Ship going along well. We have bad work to get our food cooked, as the stove is too small, and out of repairs. The vituals are only poor at present. The beef and pork are too salt and hard to be relished much, but is the worst, some of it been like wood.

June 21ˢᵗ Weather fine. We have two Saturdays in this week, as we gain a day in sailing eastward. Ship is going along well. She has sailed 243 since yesterday noon till to day at noon.

We are in Lat 51°13' Lon 173°71'. There is a flute and accordion been played together, with not the best of harmony, but all helps to pass the time away.

The following is a scale of weekly provisions:

2nd class passengers:

2lbs of preserved soups or meat. 3lbs of salt beef or pork, ½ lb of salt or preserved fish, 3½ lbs of flour, ½ lb of rice, ½ pint of split peas, ¼ lb of suet, 1lb of preserved potato, ½lb of oatmeal, ½lb of raisins, ½ lb of butter, 1lb of sugar, ½ of jam, 3 ounces of tea, 4 ounces of coffee or cocoa, ½ pint of vinegar or pickles, ½ ounce of mustard, ¼ ounce of pepper, 21 quarts of water, 6 ounces of lime juice, one dram of spirits daily to each adult male passenger, and one bottle of beer or ale to each adult female passenger weekly.

Third cabin weekly scale of provisions:

1lb of preserved soups or meat. 3lbs of salt beef or pork, 3lbs of flour, ½ lbs of preserved potatoes, ½ lb of rice, ½ lb of oatmeal, ¾ pint of peas,
¼ lb of suet, ½ lb of raisins, ½ lb of butter or jam, ½ lb of sugar, 2 ounces of tea, ounces of coffee or cocoa, ½ pint of vinegar or pickles, ½ ounce of mustard, ¼ ounce of pepper, 2 quarts of water, 6 ounces of lime juice. The quantity of biscuits is not limited, no waste is allowed.

June 22nd Weather dull. Distance since yesterday noon, 195 miles, Lon 168.

June 23rd Weather dull and cold with light showers of snow. We are in Lat 52° 20' Lon 161°44'. Distance since yesterday, 239 miles.

June 24th Weather clearer this morning. Slight quarrels amongst the passengers, respecting the sharing of provisions allowed by the ship. Lat 53°11' Lon 161°53' West. Distance run since yesterday noon 183 miles. In the afternoon weather very dull.

June 25th Weather dull and cold. Ships position Lat 52° 57'South, Lon 150°51'. Distance run since yesterday noon, 220 miles. In the evening light showers of snow.

June 26th Very cold with snow. Lat 54o36' Lon144o22' Distance 232 miles.

June 27th Cold. Gymnastics going on. Lat 55o9' Lon137o56' Distance 224 miles.

June 28th Things going on as usual. Lat 55o41' Lon131o26' Distance 226 miles. Ship going well at present.

June 29th Weather very stormy last night. This morning showers of snow falling, sun shining at intervals.

June 30th Weather very rough through last night. The tin pots and pans rattling where about in style. Ship in Lat 57o56' S Lon 116o23' Distance 223 miles. Weather very stormy last night. Ship in Lat 58o20' Lon 108o80' Distance run 257 miles. Weather very dull and cold today.

July 2nd Weather as usual, very little daylight at present. The Sun rises very little above the horizon at this season. Lat 57o36' Lon 101o9' Distance 240 miles. Ship going slowly at present. All on board in good health, excepting one or two in the second cabin.

July 4th Dull and cold. Ship in La 58o15' Lon 86o14' Distance 229 miles.
This afternoon we sighted two icebergs. The air felt very cold while passing them.

July 5th Ship in Lat 58º13' Lon 77º56' Distance run 263 miles. Wind from the north.

Some of the live stock are killed, now and then, to save them from dying with the extreme cold.

July 6th We sighted a brig at 7 o'clock this morning. She was supposed to be a South American vessel.

July 7th Weather damp. Ship going along well. Lat 57º2' Lon 72º6' Distance 202 miles.

July 8th Weather cold. Ship in Lat 56º34' Lon 64º21' Distance 254 miles. We have got round Cape Horn.

July 9th Weather clear. Ship going along smoothly. All sails set Lat 55º48' Lon 58º14' Distance 210 miles.

July 10th Weather fine. Ship in lat 54º14' Lon 51º0' Distance 267 miles.

July 11th Weather damp. We saw a beautiful iceberg this morning, in Lat 51º41' Lon 45º47' Distance 241 miles.

July 12th Weather cold. We saw an iceberg last night, and one today. Ship in Lat 49°0' Lon 45°7' Distance 189 miles.

July 13th Weather dull. Wind from north. Things going on as usual. Ship in Lat 45°44' Lon 39°38' Distance 249 miles.

July 14th Weather fine. We are going along gaily. Devine service in the form of reading prayers. I had a good wash all over this morning. Ship in Lat 42°14' lon 36°13' Distance 261 miles.

July 15th We are becalmed, in Lat 42°14' Lon 36°13'. Distance since yesterday noon, 154 miles. In the evening the moon shining bright.

July 16th Weather stormy this morning. Wind right ahead. We are in Lat 38°57' Lon 29°0' Distance 200 miles. In the evening ship going along with a faint wind.
One of the crew is in irons, for neglect of duty.

July 17th Weather fine. Wind fair. We are going along in the right course.

July 24th Weather dull. We sighted two vessels outward bound.

July 26th Weather fine and warm. We are in the Tropic of Capricorn, Lat 21°14' Lon 25° 24' Distance 190 miles. In the evening weather squally, with heavy showers of rain.

July 27th Weather very fine. We are going along well to day. All sail spread to the breeze. We are in the trade winds. Lat 19°4' Lon 25°46' Distance 132 miles.

July 28th Weather fine. Ship going well. We saw some flying fish to day. Lat 15°15' Lon 26°11' Distance 130 miles.

Passenger has a fit

July 29th Weather squally. Some time through last night, three striding sail booms were carried away during one of these squalls. We are Lon 26º40' Lat 11º36' Distance 224 miles. Weather very warm between decks. One of the passengers of the third cabins took a fit. We expect to be across the line by Thursday, if the wind holds as at present. At night weather very warm and very wet.

July 30th Weather very fine. We sighted a small vessel this morning. She was supposed to be a trader on the South American coast. There are a great many flying fish in these latitudes. To day we are in the Lat 8º19' Lon 27º15' Distance 194 miles.

July 31st Weather fine. We saw an immense quantity of flying fish. Ship in Lat 6º0' Lon 27º44' Distance 141 miles. The Sun is setting very beautiful this evening.

Aug 1ˢᵗ Weather warm. We sighted a vessel this morning. She proved to be a French barque, outward bound. She hoisted her ensign. We are in Lat 2o23' Lon 28o2' Dist? In the evening, singing on the deck. There is a fine, strong breeze, blowing in our favour, which we expect will carry us across the line.

Aug 2ⁿᵈ Very warm. We crossed the line at 2 o'clock this morning. The air was very close in our berths, so I turned out and had a bath, which was very refreshing.

Aug 3ʳᵈ Warm. Ship in Lat 1o30' North Lon 28o23'West, distance 232 miles. In the evening sports going on among the crew, to commemorate the crossing of the line.

Aug 4ᵗʰ Warm. A fine breeze blowing. A good many passengers slept on deck last night, as the air is so hot below. We are in Lat 4o10' Lon 28o20', distance 130 miles.

Aug 5ᵗʰ Weather dull and damp. I slept on deck last night. To day we saw a very large fish jump out of the water. The length of this fish was about 12 feet, and appeared to be about 3 tons weight. It jumped about 8 feet above the water and fell with a great crash into the water again. We sighted a ship. She was ahead of us. The air is very close between decks. Weather wet on deck. Ship going slowly at present.

Aug 6th Weather, showers all day. At night weather cleared up a little. We had a fine breeze for a short while but, at 11 o'clock, we were becalmed. Ship in Lat 7°54' Lon 27°55', distance 174 miles.

Aug 7th Very warm. We are still becalmed. The Sun is right over head at noon. There no birds to be seen in these latitudes. There are a few fishes sporting about the ship. Some parties are trying to catch them, but to no purpose.

Aug 8th Weather as usual. Ship going slowly. We are Lat 12°15' Lon 28°54', distance 105 miles. In the afternoon we passed a vessel so close that the Captain was able to speak with their Captain. Her name was the Joseph Fletcher of, and from, London, and bound for New Zealand. She had a great many passengers on board. They were supposed to be Government emigrants. They had been 23 days out. The Captain of her told us that peace was proclaimed. We were all glad to hear that news.[16]

Aug 9th Weather fine. A light breeze blowing. We are in Lat 12°55' Lon 30°54', distance127 miles. At night the breeze fell off. The air is very hot and sultry between decks. All of us wishing keenly for to be landed at our destination.

Aug 10th Weather very hot and calm. Our good ship is drifting astern a little. There are neither birds nor fishes to be seen. Lat 13°11' Lon 31°35', distance run 43 miles. In the afternoon we saw a good many

---

[16] The Crimean War (1853-1856) a military conflict between Russia and an alliance of England, France, the Ottoman Empire and Sardinia.

fishes. They were about the size of salmon. They were bounding out of the water, with the agility of a hare. They are called by the sailors, skipjacks.

There is not a breath of air stirring. One of the ships' boats was lowered into the water. The Captain and mate, with two of the midshipman, got into her and rowed around the ship once or twice. In the

evening two of the sailors were bathing in the sea. Just as they were busy, the first mate came out and warned any more from going over, as he had the power to prevent them.

At night, the moon shining very clear upon the glassy water. At 8 o'clock we saw a beautiful meteor shoot along the sky. The light it gave was so intense as almost to outshine the light of the moon. It most resembled an immense sky rocket. All on board owned they had never seen such a sight.

There is no sign of wind yet. Air is warm as ever.

Aug 11th Weather a little cooler this morning. A light breeze blowing. We are in what is called the North East Trade Winds. Toward night, the winds freshened. All parties in better spirits. The air is more pleasant in our sleeping berths. We are in hopes that we will see old England in about a fortnights time, if the wind holds good.

Aug 12th Weather fine. We had a strong breeze all through last night. Ship, at present, is going at 10 knots per hour, but she is not in the right course. The needle of the compass dips very much toward the north. We are in Lat 15°42' Lon 34°1', distance 190 miles.

Aug 13th Weather very fine. We are going along well, but rather out of our course. The rats are rather troublesome, as they run about our berths at night. One of them put it's foot into one of our mess mates mouth, while he lay in bed. They are drawn to our berth by the provisions, which we keep in an empty bed space. We are in Lat 18°58' Lon 35°18', distance 209 miles.

Aug 14th A good breeze blowing. We are out of the Tropic of Cancer. Ship in Lat 25°23' Lon 38°29', distance 268 miles. In the evening we sighted a barque going the same course as us. We are in Lat 28°23' Lon 39°33', distance 131 miles. In the later part of the day, we sighted other two vessels at a great distance.

Aug 16th Weather fine. A light breeze from north east. We are at present in the Gulf Stream, which travels to the eastward at about

2 or 3 knots per hour. There are large quantities of seaweed carried along by the current. Distance 70 miles.

Aug 17th Weather as usual. Ship in Lat 30°29' Lon 41°39', distance 142 miles.

Aug 18th We are going very slow to day. Weather still warm. In the evening, a fine Sun set.

Aug 20th Weather wet though last night. This morning we had thunder and lightning, wind and rain. We passed a ship. She was an American barque. Our Captain signalled her. There is a light, favourable breeze. Ship in Lat 35°11' Lon 40°59', distance 106 miles.

Aug 21st A fair wind going gaily along. There are a good many Mother

Carey's Chickens[17] following the ship. We are in Lat 36°59' Lon 38°44', distance 149 miles.

Aug 22nd A strong breeze from the West. Ship spinning along quick. We saw some Bottled Nosed Whales at a distance.

---

[17] A folklore name for the European Storm Petrel.

Aug 23rd Weather dull. We are rather out of our course. We passed a ship very close this morning. Our Captain hailed her. She was from Algoa Bay, near the Cape of Good Hope.

Her name was The Corsairs Bride. She was 53 days out. After leaving her astern, we saw another vessel right ahead. We also sighted the Western Islands, on our lee bow. Lat 40º24' Lon 31º15', distance 229 miles.. In the afternoon we passed the vessel we saw ahead. She was a Dutch barque, from Batavia to Hamburg. In the evening a heavy dew falling.

Aug 24th Wind from the east, which is right against us. All parties in low spirits. We have run 164 miles since yesterday at noon. We saw a lone vessel to day. She was at a great distance. She was supposed to be a steam vessel, bound to America. At night, the wind more favourable. We saw a large flock of birds fly past our ship.

Aug 25th Weather fine. Ship on her right course, sailing at 6 knots per hour. All on board in rather better spirits (the state of the spirits is a very good index to the progress the ship is making toward completing the voyage, which is now very tedious)

Aug 26th Weather fine. We saw a few birds to day.

Aug 27th Weather calm. We sighted a vessel at a distance. This afternoon we saw two Bottle Nosed Whales. They were about 14 feet long. They came close to the ship. At night the wind freshened. All on board keen to be on shore. All parties in good health, at present. At night we saw two large fish close under the ships bow. They are called Thrashers.

Aug 28th Weather calm. We sighted a vessel at a distance, on the weather bow. We are in Lat 44°23' Lon 21°23', distance 53 miles since yesterday noon. In the afternoon a light breeze. Weather looking unsettled. There are a good many birds around the ship.

Aug 29th Weather dull. A light breeze all day. At night weather damp. Ship in Lat 45°9' Lon 18°49', distance run 124 miles

Rats on board

Aug 31st Weather fine. We are going slowly, at 10 this morning. The wind changed to the westward, and blew a good breeze. A vessel in sight ahead. We are in Lat 45°59' Lon 16°39', distance 108.

In the afternoon there was a rat hunt. There was a nest found, with five young ones in it. They were soon committed to the deep. At four o'clock a good breeze sprung up. This put all in good spirits. There were some very heavy squalls through last night. Our good ship trembled in every part. We all expect this to be the last Saturday on board.

Aug 31st Weather fine. Our ship going along well. We are in Lat 46o45' Lon 12o27', distance run 177 miles.

Sept 1st Weather fine. Ship has been going well in the night. This morning the crew commenced to get the cable out. All parties in high spirits. A good many parties intend to land at the land's end, if they can get the chance.

Sept 2nd We sighted land at 6 o'clock in the morning. We saw the Scilly light(house) first, 2 the Lizard(lighthouse), 3 the Eddystone(lighthouse),. Next, the Start Point(lighthouse).

England at last

Sept 3rd Weather calm. All parties in low spirits, as usual in calms. There are a good many vessels of various sizes around us. They will not reach land till near midnight. At 10 o'clock at night a good breeze. We are in the English Channel. A good many vessels in sight. We are going along well with a fine wind.

There is a letter bay hanging up in the first cabin for passengers and crew, to put letters in to send on shore with the mail bags, in the pilot boat.

The main part of the first cabin passengers intend going ashore in the first boat that may come alongside. All is bustle on board, at present, and likely to continue so till we get landed.

It is very hard to be so near land and cannot get ashore.

Toward evening, the Captain signalled for a pilot boat. She soon bore down upon us, and put a pilot on board us. As soon as the pilot got on board, all hands surround him and began asking questions. Some how long the Royal Charter had been arrived, others how long the Walmer Castle had been in port, and many the questions of like nature. The pilot said the Royal Charter had arrived after a passage of

79 days (a long time for steam vessel). Of the Joseph Jarret (the vessel which left Melbourne the same day as us), there has been no tidings.

The mail bags were got into the cutter. There were 22 bags full of mail. About 28 passengers (first, second and third class) got on board the cutter, with most of their luggage. The most of them intend to proceed to London and await the arrival of the ship. The nearest land to us, at present, is Dartmouth, which is about 10 miles off. The passengers pay 20 shillings per head. In the afternoon a light breeze sprung up from the westward.

There was soon a cutter vessel off from the shore. She took about 30 passengers from the ship to the land. When she left the ship, all hands gave thrice cheer.

After this, the crew commenced to get some more cable up, lest it should be required before arriving at the far end. We are, at present, of Portland. The weather is very fine. This afternoon a very large steamship passed us. She appeared to be about 250 feet long and was a fine model. She was propelled by a screw. She carried the Hamburg flag. There were a few passengers on board.

Weather still calm. In the evening, a light breeze blowing.

Sept 4th Weather fine. A cool breeze blowing. We are off St Catherines Light, Isle of White. It is a fine sight. There are numerous vessels gliding about the Channel. If this breeze continues, we expect to be at the Downs tonight, where a steam tug is in waiting to tow us up the Thames. Wind and tide is against us at present. We are tacking about, and trying to weather Beachy Head, which is close to Brighton. A fine looking place from the sea. The coast all along here is very bold and rocky with, here and there, a fine bay.

We passed a ship of war to day. Towards evening a large boat came alongside. A good many passengers got onboard of her, and set of for Brighton, which lay about 5 miles off. At night a light on Beachy Head. It was a revolving light. The wind blowing fresh.

Sept 5th Weather fine. We are round Beachy Head and are, at present, off Folkstone, and a small place called Sand Gate. This is a very pleasant part of the English coast. From Folkstone, to the southward for a few miles, the coast is low and is guarded by a number of small towers armed with 3 guns each. A ship of war is generally stationed off this part of the coast.

On the northward of Folkstone, the coast is more bold and rocky. The rocks are composed of chalk and are about 220 feet high. These are well suited to resist the landing of an enemy. The harvest seems to be complete in this part of the country. The air feels very cool to day.

So ends this.

Epilogue

At about the time of completing the original transcription of this journal in 2013, by coincidence I was contacted by Kara Oosterman, a genealogy researcher from New Zealand.

She was tracing her own family tree.

Kara informed me that Henry Morrison, after returning to England in 1856, migrated to Napier, New Zealand in 1862 as a boat builder, with his wife Anne (nee Elliott) and baby son, John Elliot. The young family were to have a further three children after arriving.

John Elliot later migrated to Australia with the treasured journal in his possession, eventually handing it down to his son, then my grandfather and then my eldest uncle.

Henry's second eldest son, James, stayed in New Zealand to become Kara's great grandfather.

Turns out Kara was my 3rd cousin!

Kara was also able to provide me with invaluable information on Henry's further movements after his journal was written, his family lineage and archival photos of Henry and his descendants. I was mostly grateful to discover that I was part of an unknown larger family in New Zealand.

Sadly, in 1866, at the age of only 36, Henry was killed at the battle of Omarunui, near Napier, North Island, New Zealand. His fellow rifle volunteers so moved by his loss that they erected quite an impressive headstone in his honour.

Hopefully his memory also lives on in the writings recorded here.

IN MEMORY OF
HENRY MORRISON
WOUNDED IN ACTION
AT OMARUNUI
ON THE 12TH OCTOBER 1866
BORN JULY 30TH 1830
DIED OCT. 26TH 1866
AGED 36 YEARS.

ERECTED BY
THE OFFICERS AND MEN OF HIS COMPANY
THE NAPIER RIFLE VOLUNTEERS
TO MARK THEIR SENSE OF HIS COURAGE
AND WORTH.

ALSO
ANN MORRISON
WIFE OF THE ABOVE
DIED 13TH AUG 1909 AGED 75 YEARS